MO' DIRTY

STILL STUNTIN'

MO' DIRTY

STILL STUNTIN'

DARRELL KING

www.urbanbooks.net

Mo' Dirty © copyright 2008 Darrell King

ISBN- 13: 978-1-60162-068-2
ISBN- 10: 1-60162-068-3

First Printing August 2008
Printed in the United States of America

10 9 8 7 6 5 4 3 2 1

This is a work of fiction. Any references or similarities to actual events, real people, living, or dead, or to real locales are intended to give the novel a sense of reality. Any similarity in other names, characters, places, and incidents is entirely coincidental.

Distributed by Kensington Publishing Corp.
Submit Wholesale Orders to:
Kensington Publishing Corp.
C/O Penguin Group (USA) Inc.
Attention: Order Processing
405 Murray Hill Parkway
East Rutherford, NJ 07073-2316
Phone: 1-800-526-0275
Fax: 1-800-227-9604

Chapter 1

"Hood-rich Niggas"

Leon McBride had long since left the comfort of the witness protection program after the 1994 arrest and conviction of Marion "Snookey" Lake and the other members of the infamous Dirty South Syndicate. He originally had been given a new identity and was sent packing out west to New Mexico, where he spent three bittersweet, homesick years before returning to the Deep South in '98. There he spent another seven years down in Jackson, Mississsppi, and enjoyed a successful run as the minister of a local Baptist church.

Now it was 2005, and the pastor had returned to his beloved Savannah, Georgia to live for good. He'd even managed to open up a brand-new church near Bull Street, called Spaulding Baptist. The new white-and-blue house of worship boasted a large raucous congregation of 788 loyal parishioners and a forty-five-man choir, arguably the best in all of Savannah.

During the humid summer Sundays the fifty-two-year-old preacher could still deliver the word with force and vigor, causing the parishioners (especially the lovely young women) to swoon in the spirit. He still had a hidden lust for flesh that bordered on obsession and simply couldn't resist the temptation of bedding down the sanctuary's choice vixens, be they married or single. He wasn't married himself but shared a luxury cottage with his long time fiancée, Collette Briggs, in the exclusive Kingsford Plantation, an expensive gated community. Yet the skirt-chasing pastor often rented costly rooms at the Marquis de Sade Inn out on Fripp Island, where he could find adequate time to fully indulge in all his sinful fantasies.

Still, McBride knew that without the armed protection of the feds, he had to be extra careful traveling the streets of Savannah. Though Snookey Lake was currently serving time and Mafia don Alberto Cellini was said to be overseas, he realized that criminals had long and keen memories, and that neither prison bars nor thousands of miles of ocean could prevent them from extracting revenge if they chose to. He, however, continually convinced himself that as long as he kept a low profile and stayed away from drug dealers and their wares he'd be just fine.

Besides, he had his trusty armor-bearing brothers, Luke and Wallace, to watch his back, even to kill for him if need be. And with the convictions having been well over a decade ago, there was little chance that any hoodlums loyal to the old Dirty South Syndicate would be left on the streets of Savannah or anywhere else. For this reason Pastor McBride could often be found cruising darkened streets of the city with one or more of his girlfriends, dining at the top eateries, or catching a play or two at the civic center every Wednesday night after Bible study.

Either of his two armor bearers would secretly bring one of the pastor's young lovers to his chambers well after the other members had left the building for the night. They would then chauffeur the amorous couple to their Fripp Island love nest, with its huge oak shade trees, bubbling fishponds, and well-mowed courtyards.

The inn's exterior property provided a touch of vintage Southern charm to the gorgeous hotel. On Wednesday nights, a live jazz band entertained smitten couples out on the enormous patio, where they sat cuddled together at candlelit tables or danced cheek to cheek in the open courtyard below the silvery light of the full Georgia moon.

There, beneath the dark shadows of the oak limbs, Pastor McBride sipped on White Zinfandel and dined on fried catfish, okra, and Spanish rice, stealing a sultry kiss or two between bites. The pastor and his lover, the beautiful eighteen-year-old elder daughter of the choir director, became increasingly more passionate with their kisses every time their lips met. Surely in due time they would leave the patio to retire to their appointed room to enjoy a night of lovemaking.

By 10:30 the next morning, McBride and his teen sweetheart showered, dressed, and left the Marquis de Sade Inn cuddling and caressing in the back seat of a white limo driven by Brother Wallace as they left their dirty little secrets behind on Fripp Island.

Little did Pastor McBride know, he wasn't the only one heading back to Savannah from the island hideaway.

Trailing the long white limo, about two cars behind,

was a Silver Volvo S80. The well-groomed driver picked up a small black cell phone and pressed TALK. Almost immediately, a female voice answered at the other end.

"Ms. Briggs, it's Detective Lionel. I've got a lead on your fiancé. At this moment he's leaving Marquis de Sade. We're crossing the Stonewall Jackson Memorial Bridge. I have over twenty photos for you to look over also. Yeah, he's been up to no good, I'm afraid."

Without speaking, Collette Briggs gently flipped her cell phone shut and walked slowly to the front door. She paused briefly in the doorway, sighing deeply before making her way down the stairs and to the navy blue Jeep Grand Cherokee that awaited her in the circular cobblestone driveway out front. She reached down into her purse to remove a large wad of cash, passed it through the driver's side window to the scowling, cornrow-wearing youth sitting behind the wheel immersed in the throbbing tunes of T.I.

The young man politely took the money from the church lady's outstretched hand and counted it to be certain that it was all there. Then he put the Jeep in DRIVE, after replacing the T.I. disc with Trick Daddy, and slowly cruised past the gigantic wrought iron gate and disappeared down the street into the traffic beyond.

As Ms. Briggs stood in the driveway dressed in her flowing satin nightgown, she felt both guilt and supreme satisfaction for what she'd just done.

The Spaulding Baptist Church would be the pastor's first stop after dining on a light breakfast at the Old Country Buffet restaurant just before placing his playmate in a taxicab to take her home.

The young man pulled up on Bull Street around 1:45 PM and waited patiently outside of the church entrance. He let the Jeep idle gently as he put it in park and rolled up the windows, blasting the interior air conditioning units because the June heat was a blistering ninety-five degrees outside. He opened the glove compartment and removed a sturdy chrome 9 mm Glock handgun with a fully loaded clip that extended slightly beneath the handle. Smiling, he slowly attached a silencer onto the muzzle of the weapon and reclined his seat as he surfed through his cell phone's stored number settings to decide on which girl he'd settle down with later that night after he'd taken care of the day's business affairs.

There were few pedestrians out and about on this particular day, which was ideal, because daylight shootings often brought witnesses, at least those bold enough to testify.

The young man behind the wheel was no stranger to murder. He'd killed many people before—male, female, young, and old. It didn't matter one way or the other to him, and he had no problem offing witnesses. Today, however, everything seemed to be working out perfectly.

By 2:26 PM, Ms. Briggs received the phone call she both dreaded as well as impatiently awaited. Her would-be husband, Pastor Leon McBride, was dead. He and his chauffeur, Brother Wallace, had been shot multiple times as they stepped out from their parked limousine and climbed the steps toward the entrance of the sanctuary.

Many people wanted the womanizing preacher dead for one reason or another, but Peter "Whiskey" Battle had done it for the money. Both the incarcerated druglords as well as the pastor's very own betrayed fiancée had paid him handsomely to have Leon McBride eliminated.

A day later Whiskey drove back home to Peola to pick up the prison gang's portion of the money for the McBride hit. The two-and-a-half-hour drive from Savannah to Peola seemed like mere minutes, the way Whiskey was balling up Interstate 44.

First order of business was to meet up with David Ambrosia at West Peola's posh and popular nightclub, 95 South. Ambrosia had taken over the club after his brother Lee was murdered in '92. The nightclub was a favorite weekend hot spot for Peola's young adults and drew multitudes of celebrities, especially hip-hop stars. Ludacris, Jay-Z, and Snoop Dog were just a few of the luminaries who could be seen there on any given Friday or Saturday night. And local up-and-coming Peola lyricist, ATL Slim, was a fixture at the club and often performed live before sold-out audiences on summer weekends.

Whiskey knew how much his niece, Peaches, enjoyed live shows featuring rappers, so he stopped at his older sister's house to scoop her up. Peaches enjoyed the atmosphere of the lively nightclub, especially when her favorite entertainers walked about the VIP section and mingled freely with the little people like herself.

Whiskey, close friend and business partner of David Ambrosia, was a frequent visitor of the club and always received food and drinks on the house whenever he stopped by, but he'd recently limited his visits because he didn't particularly care for the place that much anymore. The clientele had become much younger, with more patrons in their late teens than years earlier, and their rowdy behavior brought about the need for more bouncers, which slowly eroded the easygoing surroundings he had become accustomed to. He also disliked the new manager Ambrosia had hired to oversee the weekly activities of the facility.

Leona McIntosh, a recently divorced forty-six-year-old mother of three from Brooklyn, New York, poured all of her energy into her young daughters and her career. After graduating from New York University with a master's degree in business, she managed the world-famous Apollo Theater and Radio City Music Hall, making her no stranger to the world of entertainment. Leona was a shrewd, oftentimes cutthroat employer. She brought 95 South a sixty-five percent increase in total revenue, and an eighty percent increase in patronage since given the position a year earlier.

But it was the cold, unforgiving methods Leona used to handle her staff that Whiskey disliked. She was an absolute asshole as a boss and ran the club like some third world dictator, firing even long-term employees for infractions as minor as missing a spot of dust on the bar counter. Whiskey didn't feel her one bit and wasn't planning on staying long.

As Peaches mingled with a few of her college friends near the crowded bar, Leona, with an outstretched hand and bubbly smile, approached Whiskey from behind the doorway leading to the VIP section. "Hello, Mr. Battle? I'm Leona McIntosh, the manager here. Mr. Ambrosia unfortunately can't be here to meet with you this evening due to a pressing business matter he had to attend to out of town. He sends his apologies and promises to phone you as soon as he returns later in the week. However, if you cannot wait until then, he suggested that you take a flight out to LA. He also asked that I tell you he'd be more than happy to pay for a round-trip ticket for you. If that's what you decide, he would like for you to catch the 12:30 AM red-eye flight out to LAX. Be sure to fly South-western. A first-class ticket will be waiting. Is that satis-factory for you, or no?"

"Yeah, that'll work." Whiskey swigged down a shot of tequila and lime.

"Great," Leona squealed. "Mr. Ambrosia will have a limo waiting for you at the airport when you arrive. Check it out. If I'm not mistaken, he'll be at the roast for Eddie Murphy, so you'll be riding with Gabrielle Union and Halle Berry. Now ain't that a blip? Afterwards, you guys are staying in Beverly Hills with one of Mr. Ambrosia's business associates."

Whiskey could tell that the manager was exaggerating a bit, but it didn't matter to him. This trip was nothing more than a business trip, a journey to receive monies due, not a vacation. "A'ight then. Let me take my niece home 'cause she ain't got a ride," he said, rising up from the barstool.

"What? Are you kidding me? You're like family to Mr. Ambrosia. I'm certain he'd want to see your niece safely home after we close for the night, and so would I. Be-sides, look at her and her girlfriends out on the dance floor. The place is jumping, and there are cute guys all over. She's having a ball. You'd totally ruin what's turn-ing out to be a wonderful night if you took her away now. I'll make sure she gets home right after we shut things down, I promise."

"Yeah, yeah, yeah. You just make sure she don't get too happy ordering all them apple martinis, a'ight?"

Whiskey left the club, while his niece, oblivious to his silent departure through the packed dance floor and right out the front door, danced the night away.

Later that night, he caught the red-eye from Peola's Burrell National Airport to the bustling LAX. After a light meal and a few glasses of champagne, he dozed off comfortably in his plush airline seat for most of the cross-country three-hour flight.

When the plane finally landed, he was a little upset because he'd just missed the best part of Martin Scorsese's *Casino*, only catching the part when Joe Pesci's character, Nicky Santoro, was beaten to death by baseball bat-wielding wiseguys. He sighed out loud as he rose from his seat to remove his belongings from the overhead luggage compartment. He never could finish watching that damn movie. Something always prevented him from seeing it to the end.

Around 4:45 AM PST, the limousine, by no means occupied with Hollywood hotties, drove into the curved driveway of an enormous Beverly Hills mansion. Once Whiskey stepped out from the rear of the elegant vehicle, he could literally see the entire expanse of La-La Land, its lights twinkling in the distance. The Hollywood sign glowed like a lone sentry on top of a hill, as helicopters fluttered across South Central, shining their searchlights in an attempt to apprehend wanted gang members.

As Whiskey walked toward the front door, a smiling David Ambrosia, flanked by two scantily clad dimes and with a half-empty bottle of Moet in his hand, approached him.

After a brief reunion of laughter, embracing, and playful banter between the two, Ambrosia welcomed Whiskey into a magnificently furnished mansion, leading him along an intricately designed, winding staircase that spiraled nearly three floors up from the bottom foyer, and showed his weary, jet-lagged homie his room. Then he gave his good-night daps and returned to the lower regions of the manor to his female companions.

In the spacious, Las Vegas-themed bedroom was a full-size refrigerator filled with several cases of imported and domestic beer and dozens of packaged frozen TV dinners. An actual miniature kitchen area held a microwave oven, and a large chestnut table with a metal bucket filled with ice and a large bottle of California Merlot.

Right before he turned in for the night, Ambrosia text messaged Whiskey to meet him at 1:30 PM downstairs in the main dining room for lunch.

It didn't take long for sleep to overcome the exhausted Georgian, who slept soundly past one.

It was 3:25 PM, and his host had long since dined and left the premises by the time Whiskey showered and dressed and came downstairs to an empty dining room, except for the housekeeping crew tidying up the area for dinner later that night.

The house chef, a spry old Venezuelan woman around sixty or so, prepared him a turkey breast sandwich that quickly proved to be filling. Afterward he proceeded to the outdoor pool area in the back, where sounds of splashing water and the giggle and laughter of bikini-clad beauties drew him like moth to a flame.

Once there, he wasn't disappointed with the bubble-butt sistas mingling with leggy blondes and buxom Latinas poolside. Some tanned themselves while stretching their taut, young figures along colorful pool chairs and reading the latest gossip mags behind dark sunshades. Others splashed about playfully in the clear, turquoise water of the pool as they hit a big, bouncy inflated ball back and forth between them.

Whiskey smiled devilishly as he took in the scenery, stroking his strong chin in expectation of a sexually gratifying night. Only a suitcase filled with neatly stacked benjamins could top fucking the shit out of a sexy-ass broad, especially the raunchy, no-holds-barred nymphos from Southern California. He'd had one or two in his day, and their bedroom skills proved to be among the best he'd experienced.

As he stood in the rear of the pool area dressed in silk Bermuda shorts and a Versace shirt, he sipped on a tall glass of Long Island Iced Tea he'd been given by a voluptuous, caramel-complexioned lifeguard he'd engaged in a brief, flirtatious discussion. When she relinquished her post atop the diving board, an equally stunning female took her place in the white chair overlooking the pool.

While mesmerized by the sheer number of hot-bodied beauties surrounding him, a hand fell upon his shoulder, breaking his lust-filled daydream. It was none other than his boy David.

"It's a whole lotta bad-ass bitches out here today, huh?" Ambrosia said in his cool Georgian twang. "If you ain't careful, you might fall in some pussy. Know what I'm sayin', Whiskey?"

As always, the baller was looking fresh in a khaki Phat Farm short set, matching Nike sneakers, and a glistening platinum herringbone chain that adorned his neck. The pleasant aroma of his $500 imported Italian cologne hovered in the dry Californian air around them like an aura of sweet-smelling raisins. The boy was still a boss player.

"Don't worry 'bout these hoes. They'll be ripe for the pickin' later on. You already know bidness befo' pleasure, playa. I need fa you ta meet some of my folks, a'ight?"

Four thugs in their twenties, all wearing black-and-white checkered bandana shirts, creased khaki pants, and black-and-white Chuck Taylor sneakers, raised up off a tastefully remodeled 1964 Chevrolet Impala.

"DiVante, Du-Loc, Snatch Man, and G-Loc, here is my man, Pete. We call him Whiskey back home."

As they clasped hands and embraced with the usual brotherly affection shown to one another in the hood, Whiskey could tell that these cats weren't fake, wannabe gangstas. They'd put in work.

"Wassup, pimpin'?" DiVante said. His father was the late DiAngelo Lovett, the former South Central leader of the Reapers street gang who'd become a well-respected civil rights and anti-gang activist before being brutally gunned down by the very hoodlums he'd once helped organize. Everyone who was anyone in the hustle game knew the Lovett family, especially out West.

The other three bandana-wearing gangstas wore scowls on their hardened young faces and bore prison tats on their neck and forearms. Surely they had seen their fair share of violence and death. Whiskey could tell a true soldier from a fake dude by the way he walked, talked, and carried himself. Game recognized game, and both parties showed one another respect after the brief introductions.

The six young men smoked two thickly rolled blunts and discussed which woman each of them wanted to sleep with that night.

"You tryin'-a hit dis shit, dawg? Dis right here is a *sherm*. Ya know, a sherman stick, it'll go nice wit' da chronic."

Whiskey noticed through reddened eyes that everyone else was smoking the PCP-soaked cigarette. "Naw, I'm a'ight. I don't fuck wit' dat sherm shit. Plus, I gotta stay focused, ya know. Got dat bidness thing ta handle, feel me?"

"True dat," Ambrosia said, choking slightly off the acrid-smelling sherm stick before passing it on to Petey, who stood next to him. He wrapped his sinewy arms around Whiskey's shoulders. "You still tired from da flight, bro?"

"Not anymore. Took a good long nap, ate a li'l bit. I'm good for right now."

"My girl Bianca can cook her ass off, can't she?"

"Well, all I got from her was a sandwich and some fries, but hey, if she's a professional chef, I guess so."

"Dawg, ol' broad can burn," DiVante said. "I've eaten mo' than a little bit of her meals. She da bomb."

Du-Loc said, "Yeah, 'specially her chicken fajitas an' shit. Dem joints is good as a mufucka."

Whiskey stomped the remainder of the roach underfoot. "I don't really give a fuck 'bout no ol' Spanish cook an' all dat bullshit. I took a plane all da way out here for one reason and one reason only—to get my money. Feel me, Davey boy?"

"C'mon, baby, you know how I roll. I got you, dawg," Ambrosia said in his usual laid-back manner. "I got ya paper right here in this duffle bag, but my mans an' dem got a slight problem, a'ight? A problem dat dey needs yo' help to get handled, feel me? Dey got an ex-employee who tried to get outta their gang. He skipped town a li'l while ago, an' now his bitch ass is snitchin' to the feds."

"Fa sho," DiVante added.

"DiVante had this cat runnin' thangs out in Long Beach for 'bout four or five years, slangin' rocks outta at least six stash houses. Dat nigga was doin' it big, pushin' beamers, flippin' dollars like it wasn't nothing, and livin' in a four-bedroom beach house overlooking the Pacific Ocean. Then, behind some shit he fucked up, he got busted. You know what happened next, right?"

"The nigga snitched, right?"

"Bingo. But it gets deeper, 'cause that fool got roots down in da Carolinas. The feds set him up wit' a trailer down in Beaufort, South Carolina and changed his identity an' all dat type secretive bullshit, just as long as he brings down the major playas in the South Central, LA crack game. Which includes the whole Reapers gang, which, of course, is run by none other than my man, DiVante Lovett. You know good an' damn well dat we can't let my man DL go out like dat behind some fuckin' dumb-ass snitch, right?"

Whiskey took a deep gulp of Long Island Iced Tea, wiped a diamond-encrusted hand across his moist lips, and belched loudly. He stared intently at DiVante Lovett.

The handsome, rugged-looking youngster with the long, braided hair and smooth, sandy-brown complexion stared back at him through unblinking hazel brown eyes that women adored and men feared, silently awaiting an answer.

"This mufucka is due to go on the witness stand this comin' fall, around October or November. The feds gonna have him call everybody an' their mama out. Ain't no goddamn way we gonna let dis punk bitch last dat long."

"You gotta peel his cap back, homie. David done told us dat you da man when it comes ta deadin' niggas. We know da dude's livin' down in y'all's neck o' da woods an' shit. So can you take care of this light work for us or what?" Petey puffed on the powerfully narcotic sherman stick.

Whiskey finished the glass of iced tea and sat it down on a small patio table near him and turned toward Di-Vante. "Ya know what, cuz? About five years ago this dude named Nathan robbed a credit union in West Peola and got away wit' somethin' like two to three grand. He had his two cousins as his flunkies. He never did fully pay them cats what he owed dem an' even turned around an' ratted on 'em when he got his dumb ass busted a year later. Shit, da nigga even brought my name up in it, 'cause he had bought the getaway car from me before he'd pulled off the robbery. I was fuckin' pissed off and hurt at the same time, 'cause I thought Nathan was my man an' shit. But I ain't even had to get at 'im, for real, 'cause his cousin Topp shot 'im in da face comin' out of da police station on St. Patrick's Day two thousand. I'll never forget that day as long as I live. I was lucky I didn't get locked up my damn self behind dat stupid shit."

"What does that gotta do wit' anything?" DiVante asked.

"Well, what I wanna know is, why you gotta get me ta dead dis dude? I mean, y'all got thangs on lock out here an' shit, right? Everyody knows dat da Reapers run almost all of the Pacific Coast and can touch folks even in other states, so why you need me to handle ya bidness for you?"

"You gotta hear me out, playa. We got things pretty much airtight out here on our end, that's true. An', if necessary, yes, we can reach out an' touch a nigga anywhere in da country if we have to. But that would take way too long to get done, know what I'm sayin'?"

"I dunno. I guess if y'all cool wit' my man David, then we pretty much family, right?"

"Bet. David's always talkin' 'bout you, dawg. He been tellin' war stories 'bout you for so long, we feel like we know every damn thing 'bout you. An' from everything that DA been tellin' us, you a straight *G*, no doubt, an' we want you ta do dis nigga for us, cuz."

Whiskey snickered. "Well, I'm pretty sho dat you done stretched a coupla niggas out in da streets befo' ya damn self, ain't dat right?"

Snatch Man dragged deeply on yet another cigarette that he'd just soaked in a small container of PCP, exhaled a cloud of smoke, which hovered in the air above his head, then spat a thick clump of phlegm onto the ground below. "*Sheeet*, nigga, how I feel 'bout dat bitch-ass nigga, I'll murk his whole mufuckin' family, cuz, believe dat shit."

Du-Loc took the sherman stick offered to him from Snatch Man. "I'm wit' my man Snatch on dat one. I'm 'bout ready to ride on dat mark myself, for real."

Whiskey took the army-green duffle bag that Ambrosia gave him, knelt down, and quickly began flipping through the twenties, fifties, and hundreds. Once he was satisfied with the amount there, he stood and addressed the group.

"A'ight, what's dis nigga's name, and how does he look?"

"His name is Larry, but da streets know 'im betta as Gimp. He a short, fat, dark-skinned nigga wit' a pot belly and a thick-ass beard an' shit." DiVante flipped open his cell phone and scrolled through a series of photos featuring himself and other members of the Reapers, including Gimp, posing gangsta-style, brandishing weapons, forty-ounce malt liquor bottles, and wads of money spread out fan-like within their grasps. "He used ta be one of my most hard-core enforcers, handlin' business for me whenever bustas got outta line out here in da hood. He almost single-handedly kept da Bloods and Crips sets out in Watts. He'll dead a nigga without hesitation an' won't give a fuck who dey is—I'll give da nigga dat much. Since da age o' twelve he been out here on da streets grindin', an' da boy know how ta flip dem dollars, as you can see from dese here pictures an' shit. He know how to network wit' da game's biggest ballers."

"Beaufort, huh? I wonda why da feds would send a nigga all da way across da country? Well, I guess it would be understandable though," Whiskey remarked.

DiVante nodded in agreement. "The feds know dat leavin' Gimp anywhere on da West Coast, he's as good as dead. Ya know they can't afford to take dat risk, so quite naturally they gonna place him somewhere far off where they feel he won't ever be found. But, see, two things Gimp's fat ass can't resist—Naw, make that three—

pussy, money, and food. We both got da same coke con-nect, a Mexican cat outta Houston. Ya see, obviously Gimp been hittin' 'im up for some weight over the past two or three months. I heard 'bout Gimp's new place o' residence by just kickin' it on da phone one night wit' my man Chico. I bet he don't even know how much of a favor he did a nigga dat night.

"Listen to me, Whiskey, there ain't no fuckin' price dat I won't pay or can't pay so I can stop dis nigga from tes-tifying against me an' shit. Ya heard what I said, cuz? I'll pay whateva to shut Gimp's mufuckin' mouth for good.

"Da feds must not know that Gimp's been buyin' a couple o' kilos o' pure Colombian flake through one o' his new little country girlfriends that make all o' da phone calls and pick-ups for him. Da nigga's too smart to get hisself caught up a second time. But, anyway, his main girl works at a restaurant called The Toddle House. Supposedly he picks her up from there around 11:30 PM every Monday, Wednesday, and Friday night. Feds be checkin' up on him a lot, though, so you gonna have ta watch ya back. When you get back down South, hit me up on da cell and lemme know after you done peeled his wig back, and I'll wire you da cash. Ya know I'm good for it, or else David here wouldn't o' introduced you to me, right?" DiVante reached out a clenched fist and gently pounded his with Whiskey's.

Whiskey sat down on a nearby pool chair and blew kisses at two curvaceous beauties, who smiled brightly as they passed the young men en route to the opposite side of the busy pool. "I ain't got a problem wit' bustin' a cap in ya man an' all. It's all in a day's work for me, you know, but I'm gonna have to ask for thirty grand, fifteen gees up front befo' I fly back, an' another fifteen after I murk dis Gimp character for you. Is dat a'ight wit' you?"

"Like I said earlier, it's whateva, dawg. My pockets stay on swole, so money ain't an issue for me, cuz. I just want da nigga dead, that's all."

Whiskey liked what he was hearing. All the stories he'd heard about DiVante and his now dead pops Di-Angelo being gangsta and boss playas must be true if he could just come up with fifteen thousand dollars in such a short amount of time. This was surely not some weak nigga wit' short money.

"Y'all ain't gotta worry 'bout ol' Gimp fa too much longa, 'cause once I get back down South, his ass is grass." Whiskey placed the duffle bag near his chair and smiled with the realization that his best friend had set him up with a top-dollar-paying murder job with the added perk of having access to a major West Coast drug trafficker to boot. He would have to show David Ambrosia how much he appreciated his looking out.

DiVante gave Whiskey his personal cell phone number, which the Southern bad boy placed into his own cellular menu.

"Whiskey, if you complete this work like we ask you to, and mind you, I already know you will, we can have a real long business relationship makin' moves dat make money, okay? Before you leave for Georgia tomorrow night, I'll have Du-Loc drop off da fifteen gees for you around noon. I got a bitch I fucks wit' who works security at LAX. She da head o' da airport security an' shit, so she can have her staff let you slip through wit'out all da fuckin' questions as to why you travelin' wit' so much cash. 'Cause, dawg, you carryin' a li'l over twenty-seven grand, wit' the fifteen I'm puttin' up, plus da twelve you already got in ya duffle bag. So you know dem rental cops gonna trip."

"That'll work. If everything goes as planned, this fool should be long gone by the end of da week, I promise you dat much."

"I bet you he will." DiVante grinned. "After you confirm dat Gimp's dead, I'll wire ya da second payment by Western Union ."

Snatch Man eyed a thick, big-booty redbone clad in a skimpy two-piece, who blushed bashfully as she pranced by. "I know you niggas like talkin' 'bout peelin' dudes' caps back, an' money an' shit, but I'm 'bout ta hit dis pool an' fuck wit' dese bitches right now."

Whiskey rubbed his palms together in anticipation. "Shit, nigga, you ain't gotta tell me twice."

"We gonna have a lotta fun out here wit' dese hoes dis evenin', homie, so let's go on over to da bathhouse over here to da right. I already got da joint stocked wit' a bunch o' swim trunks o' all different colors and sizes, ready to wear. I even got Speedos, but don't wear dem faggot-ass joints. They strictly for da Jacuzzi action, you feel me?" David said.

The five young men followed Ambrosia along the water's edge toward the beige, stucco-colored bathhouse at the far end of the pool, nestled in between a clump of pygmy palm trees. As they entered, each one chose a spacious fitting room, where they found shelves stacked from top to bottom with neatly arranged swimwear.

DiVante playfully nudged Whiskey as they emerged from their individual dressing rooms. "Ya first time visiting LA seems ta be turnin' out quite nicely, huh, Whiskey? You been paid pretty good, an' now you 'bout ta getcha mufuckin' brains banged out by one o' dem sexy dimes out there in a minute or two. Now that's gangsta."

DiVante wasn't lying. Whiskey would never forget his first trip out West. As he walked out to the edge of the Olympic-sized pool and sat down casually at the edge of the thirteen-foot area of the pool, dangling his muscular legs into the cool, clear water, gorgeous females swam below his feet, while the other cutie pies chatted away continuously as they laid back comfortably on their poolside chairs and smiled at him flirtatiously.

A deejay began spinning a medley of West Coast gangsta hits featuring the aggressively sick tracks of Ice Cube, Snoop Dogg, and Doctor Dre, and the beauties began to sway seductively as they broke out dancing to the ghetto jams blaring loudly from the thumping bass speakers spread out around the pool. Within minutes the boys were surrounded by curvaceous, bikini-wearing sex kittens grinding on them to the West Coast classic, "California Love."

The young revelers partied well into the night, a steady flow of twenty-somethings from all around the Beverly Hills neighborhood eagerly joining in the wet and wild festivities.

Next morning's sunrise, Whiskey arose smelling of expensive imported liquor and the funk of the unbridled sexual marathon from the night before. He crawled out from under the naked, cum-stained bodies of two snoozing beach bunnies sprawled out across his broad chest and snoring loudly in a sex- and booze-induced slumber.

As the Georgia-bred enforcer stood beneath the tepid spray of the above showerhead in the luxurious mahogany-tinted marble bathroom, he could now focus solely on the job ahead—murder.

June 27th, 11:40 PM *Beaufort, South Carolina*

"Dey dat fucka go, dawg!" Lil' Shane quickly started up the engine of the rust-colored 1981 Monte Carlo, which rattled to life with a loud guttural roar. The cocaine-sprinkled marijuana blunt filled the interior of the classic vehicle with a strange, sweet-smelling psychedelic aroma, bringing about a dreamy, surreal atmosphere that briefly masked the very real drama that was about to unfold.

"Calm yo' ass down, dawg. I got dis." Whiskey placed the last three hollow-tip slugs into the magazine of the TEC-9 and stuffed it into the stock of the gun.

He'd done this type of thing many times before, so he wasn't nervous or jittery in the least. In fact, he seemed rather eager to carry out his deadly assignment.

Then he positioned himself on the passenger's seat, so that he might have leverage enough to blast his target from the open window as they cruised from across the street to the other side.

Medium in height but built like a beer barrel, Gimp was recognizable not only from his rotund form, but also from his slight limp, as he made his way from his parked SUV toward the dimly lit restaurant before him. Onward he hobbled, puffing on a smoldering Black & Mild cigar and observing the messages on his cell phone, which glowed a fluorescent green in his palm in the dark South Carolina night.

From his expensive urban wear ensemble accented by sparkling diamond jewelry upon his hands, wrists, and neck, and classic Chuck Taylor sneakers, Whiskey could see that this cat continued to rep his West Coast roots even now while deep in the heart of Dixie. He almost admired the man he was to soon kill. He smoked the blunt he held down to an insignificant roach before flicking it out the window into the darkness beyond.

Lil' Shane shut off the headlights and put the engine in neutral, letting the big car drift along the street silently, except for the softly humming engine.

As the Monte Carlo cruised down the street toward Gimp's parked truck, Whiskey stuck the muzzle of the TEC-9 out the passenger side window. The TEC-9 had incredible firepower. A mere pull of the trigger could squeeze off over a dozen murderous rounds of hot lead into some poor fool or unsuspecting crowd, always guaranteeing three or more kills and multiple injuries.

The Monte Carlo seemed to take forever to pass Gimp's big-bodied Yukon. However, once they rode past the front end of the Yukon, Gimp's corpulent form came into view. Whiskey leaned forward, allowing his upper body to protrude out the window slightly. His finger on the trigger, he steadied his gaze on the heavyset man standing a mere twenty paces away, where he'd suddenly stopped in order to scroll through his phone's digital menu more closely.

Lil' Shane whispered, "Blast his fat ass, Whiskey. He done stopped. He's standin' still for you, man."

The assault weapon held by Whiskey began rattling off a barrage of deadly shots, splitting the silence with a deafening series of *rat-a-tat-tats* accompanied by bright orange flashes of flame that erupted from the barrel.

The ex-gangbanger-turned-informant screamed out in shock and agony as dozens of hollow-tip bullets zipped through and around his wide frame. He fell backward onto the cobblestone path with a blubbery plop, his cell phone tumbling a few feet from his hands into the grass along the side of the pathway. Gimp's left leg and his right arm twitched with rapid herky-jerky movements, and as his blood pooled out onto the cobblestone, his breathing came in short, gurgling gasps.

By the time his girlfriend and her co-workers raced to the scene, he was already staring ahead, eyes wide open in death. While his lover cupped his bloody head into her arms and weeped hysterically, the other witnesses could do little but dial 9-1-1 as they caught but a brief glimpse of the fleeing Monte Carlo's red taillights speeding away down the dirt road, down the hills, and past a dark grove of palmetto trees beyond.

Chapter 2

"The Ways of a Ryder"

July 13th, 2005, 10:22 PM

Whiskey was just leaving North Peola's affluent Sorrell Dunes gated community after dropping off more than a few bags of blow to several of his well-heeled coke clients. He'd spent a little over forty minutes making rounds and came away with twelve grand. He then hopped in his Jeep Cherokee and got onto the busy Madison Highway outer loop, en route to South Peola's Hemlock Hills project.

He hadn't fed his pit bull terriers at all that day, so that his fighting dogs might be ornery and game for the bloody contests of the coming midnight hour. The controversial and brutally violent blood sport attracted dozens of ghetto youth from all over Peola's projects with their best-bred fighting pedigree canines—American pit bull terrier, German rottweiler, Japanese Akita, and English bull mastiff. The featured combatants fought oftentimes to the death, while the yelling mob bet hundreds on the outcome of the savage battles.

Dogfights were usually held on the weekends, out near Geneva Projects through the Sundance Forest and on the property of an old, abandoned farmhouse, reputedly said to have once been a part of Harriet Tubman's legendary Underground Railroad. Peola's upper-crust residents would often send associates down to the hood with several hundred dollars to place side bets on the area's top dogs.

Whiskey had learned to breed, raise, and train dogs for the pits from his older brother Leon for six years, just before he was shot to death by Peola's police during a routine traffic stop—They mistook his reaching for his car's registration as attempting to grasp a weapon. Though Whiskey had raised a variety of fighting dog breeds successfully, he specialized in the rearing of pit bulls, with which he rarely, if ever, lost matches. People came from as far away as Florida to breed their dogs with his or to buy newborn puppies from his champion fighters, and paid top dollar for these services, which could run anywhere from $800 for a puppy to $15,000 for stud services. Whiskey usually never fought his own pets, except for a select few that he would bring out to fight, to advertise the elite fighting prowess for business as well as bragging rights.

The pathway leading up to the pitting areas themselves was well guarded by armed lookouts, who only allowed walk-ins with a single ace of spades playing card with a hole punched through the middle as a part of the process to gain entry, along with ten dollars and the secret password, which would change with each passing month. Vehicles were not allowed entry, nor could any car, truck, or motorcycle penetrate the dense surrounding undergrowth of Sundance Forest anyway. Elaborate escape routes were developed, in case of a surprise police raid, which was virtually impossible for the cops to launch.

Spectators who attended these bloody affairs mostly came to bet on the dogfights alone, yet it wasn't uncommon for certain individuals to approach the presiding hustlers to solicit drugs. In fact the dogfights were, in large part, a veritable bazaar for all sorts of illicit activities. So when Paul Ballard nudged Whiskey to converse with him privately outside of the barn, away from the fierce action of the pits, he wasn't the least bit surprised.

Paul had just recently gotten out of Akron Correctional Facility after doing a six-year sentence for an armed robbery beef back in 1999. He, like most others who came home from doing time behind bars, had become noticeably larger, especially in the upper body area. He now wore thick, curly hair in long, tightly knotted dreads that flowed down to nearly a quarter of his wide, well-muscled back. His white wife-beater stretched tightly, revealing powerfully built pecs, and tapered down to display a solidly chiseled set of six-pack abs. Numerous crudely stenciled prison tattoos covered his dark, brawny arms, and his baggy jeans hung well beneath his narrow waist, showing nearly the full measure of his gray-and-black boxer shorts, and exposing the glossy, black stock of a Beretta 9 mm.

"Sup witcha, baby? Looks like the grind been treatin' you well, cuz." Paul grinned through diamond-encrusted gold teeth.

"Hey, you know how we do it down here in da Hills, dawg. Ain't nuttin' change since you been gone."

"You brought dem two pits up next, right?" Paul took a wad of rubber band-wrapped bills from his shorts and peeled off seven hundred dollars.

"Yeah, Buddah is da black-and-white male wit' da white spot in da middle o' his forehead. He fifteen an' 0, with seven kills, and dat brindle joint is Daisy. She ain't got but one eye, but she done been in over forty fights an' she ain't lost one yet. She done kilt over twenty-two dogs. Da last dog she fought an' kilt was a one hundred-pound rottie. She tore his big ass up in less than three an' a half minutes flat. Buddah's a bad mufucka, but Daisy ain't no joke. Put ya money on her."

"I know dat's right." Paul handed Whiskey seven hundred-dollar bills and turned the bottle of malt liquor he'd been drinking up to his lips for a quick swig. "I'm side-bettin' wit' you tonight, pimpin', 'cause everybody from da Hills know dat you breed da rawest dogs in Peola, for real. If they don't know—fuck 'em—they'll soon find out. Ain't dat right, Whiskey?"

"I'm always willin' ta teach a nigga a li'l som'n-som'n."

"A'ight, bet. Let's go back in an' make a li'l bit o' money, shall we? But befo' we go back in," Paul said in a more serious tone, "I gotta let you in on some shit dat's been jumpin' off out here in da hood, a'ight?"

Whiskey nodded, and both men walked back into the old, decrepit barn.

Just as they entered, Lil' Shane released Daisy into the ten-foot-wide caged-off pit. The air was filled with the sickly smell of blunt and cigarette smoke mingled with liquor and blood. The sandy floor of the baiting area was raked for several minutes after each battle, to allow the blood of the wounded or dying dogs to sink in, to prevent the upcoming canine warriors from slipping.

Daisy sprang immediately at her opponent, a powerfully built, white English bulldog, and fastened her mighty jaws with a vise-like grip onto its throat. Both mongrels tumbled about in the sand of the pit, thrashing around, snarling, yelping, and growling ferociously, while dust and blood-flecked froth flew across the miniature arena. The raucous shouts of the betting crowd grew louder as the canine combatants twisted and turned, each one trying to gain an advantage over the other to deliver a final death bite.

Paul turned to Whiskey and whispered into his ear, "I been out here hustlin' for a minute just like you, Whiskey. 'Cept, I done hooked up wit' a new connect dat's got me on a whole other level, playa. I'm 'bout to put you on to some deep shit, my nig, but only if you think you ready for it."

"It ain't a helluva lot dat can shock me, Paul. Talk to me."

"A'ight, you asked for it. Since I got out in January, I been meetin' wit' my parole officer twice a month, the first and last of each month, right. Okay, although I'm on papers an' shit, dis bitch I'm s'pose ta meet wit' each month is cool as a mufucka. Plus, she got me workin' wit' a coupla dirty cops in da department. They some down-ass dudes though. I done peeped 'em, an' they legit. They pullin' in mo' money than Snookey and dem back in da day, 'cause dey da ones bustin' all da dealers. They got our backs, though, as long as we split the dope profits fifty-fifty down da middle. Now I know dat da amount seems a li'l bit high, but hey, whatcha gon' do? Argue wit' da po-po? We stand ta gain a whole lot mo' than what you might think in da long run. Plus, dem pigs got access to da crystal meth business. Dat shit right dere is hotter than *E* pills used ta be, ya heard? We gotta get dis money, dawg, an' I know dat wit' ya help we can make even mo' than ever."

"I dunno, Paul. I don't too much trust no cops, dawg, 'specially not these dirty-ass fuckas down here in Peola. You know what dem people think 'bout us po' black folk in da hood, don't ya?" Whiskey whispered back, sneaking looks at the two dogs grappling in the swirling dust of the pit.

"Yeah, well, don't you go worryin' 'bout no sneaky ol' cracka cops, a'ight? I got things on lock wit' dem boys dem. Oh shit! Look, Daisy done got a death lock on dat bulldog's throat. Look like we gonna be 'bout a thousand dollars richa in a few, huh?"

"I told you, I don't breed losers, an' don't you ever forget it, a'ight?" Whiskey lit up a half-smoked blunt he'd just removed from his baggy denim shorts. While enjoying the slowly, creeping buzz delivered by the potent sour diesel bud, he began to reconsider his previous decision to not associate with Pete's police pals.

"Yes!" both men yelled out with joy as the pit judge forcibly removed Daisy's blood-soaked jaws from around the badly torn neck of the lifeless bulldog.

Whiskey quickly moved through the densely crowded, clamorous, and smoke-filled aisle toward the pit area, where he secured his victorious, yet battle-scarred pet and returned her to his personal dog handler, who fed her a juicy treat of raw venison before placing her in a roomy holding cage. He then met with the losing dog's owner, who reluctantly shelled out a wad of cash totaling a grand, and returned back through the liquored-up throng to his rickety bleacher seat next to Paul. Whiskey folded a knot of five hundred dollars and placed the cash to his pursed lips and kissed it gently before stashing it down into his exposed boxers.

"Thank you, my man. I can get used ta dis dogfightin' shit, 'specially if I'm winnin'. Check it out, Whiskey. Ya know who dem pigs tryin' ta get at though? Dey own boss, ol' punk-ass Mickey O'Malley an' shit."

Whiskey's eyes went wide with disbelief.

"Oh yeah, dat Mickey O'Malley been fuckin' it up for a whole lotta folk, dawg. Da only baller he even fucks wit' out here on da streets is David Ambrosia, an' ever since David moved down to Daufuskie Island, he been shittin' on every fuckin' body, cuz. Even members o' his own police force want his bitch ass dead, 'cause can't nobody make no money wit' him comin' down hard on dope dealers all over da city. Know what I mean?"

"I feel you, partna. I know how dat redneck Irish mufucka can be. He damn sho don't play fair." Whiskey shook his head. "When a man starts fuckin' wit' ya chedda, you gotta bleed his ass, no doubt."

Suddenly the clamor of the betting horde caught their attention, as a fierce Presa Canario and a vicious Japanese Tosa raged violently down in the dusty pits below.

"Now dat's da Whiskey I used to know, a straight soldier who would dead a nigga on sight. So wassup? You know you and I used to be two o' da baddest enforcers ta bust guns in all o' Peola. Remember when we used ta run wit' Dawn, Shawn, and Rae-Kwon? *Sheeet*, nigga, we use ta strike fear in bitch niggas' hearts, dawg."

"Yeah, I know, I know. It's jus', you know, a whole helluva lot different. You talkin' 'bout takin' out a fuckin' chief o' police, playa. You just can't walk up an' peel a cop's wig back like talkin' 'bout it, pimp, feel me? 'Specially not a goddamn chief o' police. C'mon now."

"Whatever, nigga. I done seen you pop plenty o' so-called high-profile cats befo', dawg. How 'bout da pastor you jus' took out over a month ago? Yeah . . . didn't know I knew 'bout dat shit, huh? Word gets out fast on da streets, you should know dat." Paul looked his friend straight in the eye without blinking, searching for some sort of reaction from him.

"Looka here, Paul," Whiskey responded with a slight tone of irritation in his voice, "I'm a hustla an' a thug wit' a gun who'll do whatever it takes ta make a dollar, an' if it means I gotta kill a mufucka, then guess what? He's as good as dead, as far as I'm concerned. 'Specially if da paper's lookin' right. I don't give a fuck who it is or what occupation da mufucka claims. Dat ain't my concern. I'll deal wit' da Lord when I go ta glory. Until then I'm gonna do me all day long." Whiskey took out yet another pre-rolled blunt and fired it up, to soothe his suddenly frazzled nerves.

"Hey, calm down, baby. I ain't comin' down on ya, dude. I'm just tryin' ta help both o' us make a little bit o' money by workin' wit' dese crackas, dat's all. Just like ol' times. 'Cept we'll be smokin' a cop dis time around. C'mon, Whiskey, don't nobody like O'Malley's fat Irish ass, no mufuckin' way. He ain't nuttin' but a white racist any ol' way. He ain't never done nuttin' for da hood or us black folks, like you said earlier. Plus, a whole lotta white boys out in West Peola losin' a shitload o' cash as we speak 'cause o' dat fat, roly-poly bitch. An' dey want his ass taken care of just as bad as da crack-slangin' niggas down here on da South Side, feel me? Besides, like I said, dem peoples done promised me over sixty grand for da hit. Shit, we can split it thirty-thirty if you want, I don't care. I'd be happy to give you fifty grand, you know dat. I'da done it my damn self, but like I said befo', I'm on papers an' shit."

Paul motioned for Whiskey to come closer, and when he did, gave him a beige-colored envelope that seemed somewhat bulky and overstuffed. "Go on, open it up. Shit, I'm dyin' ta see what dem cops blessed you wit' myself."

Whiskey slowly ripped it open and twelve hundred dollars in cash spilled out into his waiting hands. "Goddamn! Yo' li'l badge-wearin' buddies uptown really want ta off O'Malley, don't they?" Whiskey flipped the benjamins through his fingers one by one.

"Ya damn skippy, they do. An' when you pull off da job, there's plenty mo' green waitin' for ya. So is it on an' poppin' or what?"

"Tell ya boys in uniform their retainer fee is fully accepted and ol' man O'Malley should be given a nice twenty-one-gun sendoff in about a week or so, a'ight."

"How 'bout two weeks, just to be on the safe side, cuz? We don't wanna rush nuttin' unnecessarily."

"That'll work too."

"Lemme give you my cell phone number, a'ight. It's 737-324-6116."

"Cool. I got it logged into my menu. What's a good time ta holla at ya?"

"I'm always on da move an' shit. I start my day earlier than most, usually around eight. But I always check my messages throughout da day, so you can expect a call back even if you don't get me right away."

"You ever race ya bike?"

"Naw, but I'll drag race da shit outta my ol' '65 Ford Mustang. I calls her *Mustang Sally*, after the old Wilson Pickett song. I been workin' on her for over five years. She got an eight-cylinder cam, an' she ain't been beat yet. I done took hundreds off niggas out on Century Boulevard in Pemmican. Ask David, he'll tell ya hisself."

"Okay, I heard dat. Well, maybe I gotta bring my old '72 Roadrunner out da garage an' shit, so I can get some o' dat action on Century Boulevard some time. When y'all drag?"

"Mostly on Saturday nights at around one or two in the mornin'. A whole lotta cats be out there wit' their whips and their bitches. Races be 'bout a quarter-mile to a mile, but I prefer da shorter one-block races myself, you know. Lotsa money out there ta make, fuckin' wit' dem spoiled, rich kids. Dey ain't got shit else ta do but throw away dey parents' dough."

"How many races you won?"

"I'd say around 'bout six or seven. Now I'll tell you dem white boys from Canterbury Arms wit' their Ferraris and tricked-out Porsches ain't ta be fucked wit'. Sleep on dem crackas, an' you'll lose da shitty drawers off ya ass, dawg. Bring ya A game if an' when ya come out—Just a warnin'."

"Who's won da most races out on da West Side?"

"Jeremy Lattimore, da mayor's son. He drives a lemon yellow 2004 Dodge Viper. He hasn't lost a race yet."

"How many races has dis cat won altogether?"

"Shit, who knows, dawg? It's gotta be over a hundred or mo'. Now, dat I do know."

"Hmmm . . . I see. I do gotta bring my A game when I come out ta dat joint wit' da whip an' shit, huh?"

"Shit, yeah. Unless ya jus' tryin' ta throw away a couple o' hundred dollars an' whatnot. If dat's da case, shit, jus' hand da shit over ta me. I'll spend it for ya."

Whiskey grinned and threw mock jabs at his friend's ripped abdomen.

Whiskey believed in his heart that David Ambrosia had to be the one to discuss the killing of Pastor McBride with the recently freed jailbird. He wasn't necessarily upset about the whole thing, because they were all long-time pals. However, with Paul's connections caught up in the mix, he figured that discretion would be in order, until he proved that they could be trusted.

"The best car I ever raced was an '81 Ford Pinto. Man, that li'l whip could ball, you hear me?" Paul smiled as he reminisced. "My li'l brother Marion and me pimped it out and souped da engine up, and boy, we was dustin' niggas out on Madison Highway, 'specially da outer loop an' shit. You shoulda seen us. We burned a cop or two back in da day wit' dat joint. Dat ride was da shit."

"Sounds like it coulda been a winner. What da fuck happened to da joint?"

"My brother fucked around an' totaled it comin' back from South Carolina one night. I guess it was around ninety-six or ninety-seven, one o' da two. I can't quite remember now, but he jus' broke his wrist and had a couple o' scratches on his face and shit. But, other than that, he was a'ight."

The bestial growls coming from the pit caused the throng of cheering spectators to break out into a resounding roar as the great Tosa, bloodied but undeterred, pinned the equally monstrous Presa to the gore-splattered dirt of the dusty arena and delivered a fatal bite to its exposed jugular, bringing the bloody combat to an abrupt and merciful end. The Tosa's owner, along with several others who'd placed heavy wagers on his dog's odds of besting the Presa, cheered loudly and embraced each other in victorious celebration.

Paul peered down at the cell phone clipped to his denim shorts and answered the chirping device. He conversed briefly before hanging up.

"Whiskey, I gotta get up outta here, dawg. I gots dis bad-ass bitch out on da North Side, right? She jus' moved here 'bout two or three months ago from Brazil. Bitch is fatta than duck butta an' fine as shit, an' peep dis, she can't get enough sex, no matter how much dick I gives her. Believe me, I breaks da bitch back, ya hear what I'm sayin'? Plus, she got plenty money, 'cause she lives right on Sorrell Dunes Beach in da fancy li'l condos an' shit. Yeah, a freak bitch wit' long dollars. She's a keeper, for now anyway. So I'll holla at ya sometime dis week, probably Wednesday or Thursday, so we can go over dis bidness shit we discussed, a'ight?"

"Aw, c'mon, nigga. Fuck dat ho. We ain't seen each other in a minute, an' I got two more pits I'm 'bout ta put in da ring, playa. If you stick around for a while, you'll be walkin' outta here wit' well over a grand."

"Maybe next time, baby boy, but dat pussy callin' a nigga right 'bout now, cuz. An' da wood in my drawers is tellin' me dat I gotta answer dat call, so I'll holla."

"Yeah, whatever, nigga. Get ya pussy-whipped ass da fuck on." Whiskey chuckled lightly.

Then he and Paul Ballard walked outside into the humid night, complete with a hazy but starry sky hanging above the dark silhouettes of tall Georgia pines and old moss-covered oaks.

"You got my number, so I'm gonna expect a call by midweek, Whiskey, for real though, 'cause we gotta take care o' dis, seriously."

Whiskey waved his hand nonchalantly as he watched Paul walk with the flashlight-wielding sentry toward the dark forest trail and into the inky blackness of the woods ahead. He smiled and slowly returned to the din of the raucous crowd within the barn to renew the series of dogfights he'd come to bet on earlier.

Chapter 3

"Family Reunion"

Tasha had just finished preparing breakfast for her four children when her younger brother stepped through the front door a little after eleven. Whiskey's nephews, Ron, Kelly, and Barry, raced over to embrace him excitedly.

Whiskey returned the love and followed the trio into the living room, where they were busy playing video games on the PS2. He observed the violent game play of the pixilated figures on the wide-screen television and grinned as his nephews pressed frantically on the hand-held controllers while intently viewing the screen.

"What y'all li'l niggas playin'? *Grand Theft Auto*?"

"Yup. And I'm already on da fifth level right now," Ron said proudly.

"Yeah, y'all gonna put up dem damn games an' clean up my living room too. I know dat much. Now wash y'all hands and get ready ta eat breakfast."

"Pete, you want some'n ta eat? We got plenty."

"Maybe a li'l later, sis. I'm gonna just catch up on a li'l sleep an' shit 'cause I had a long night an' I'm beat dis mornin'. Where Peaches at?"

"She spent da night over at her girlfriend Ramona house. It's like dat's her second home now."

Whiskey's sister, LaTasha Battle, was a thirty-three-year-old administrative assistant for the Jefferson Davis accounting firm in Burginstown, an upstate college town populated by primarily young white-collar types. Tasha, as she was more widely known, had been a hard-working homemaker since the tender age of eleven when her mother, Maureen Battle, first began to exhibit signs of chronic substance abuse. She'd raised her two-year-old brother, Peter, while her pregnant mother ran the streets with various lovers in search of a good time in the form of a bottle of cognac, a bag of coke, or cheap sex in the backseat of a Cadillac.

Tasha and her younger brothers never knew who their biological father was, nor did their neglectful mother release information of his identity to them. But it was widely rumored among relatives as well as casual associates that the infamous New Orleans drug lord, Marion Snookey Lake, had indeed fathered the Battle trio.

The story was that during the early reign of Snookey Lake, he often visited the low country regions of South Carolina and Georgia to establish a target drug trafficking network, as well as a quick escape route out of the Crescent City when and if the ever-present FBI closed in for the kill. During one such interstate trip through southern Georgia, the Louisiana kingpin was introduced to the svelte, ruddy-complexioned knockout sitting alone cross-legged at the bar in a nightclub known as Da Juke Joint by the late Wallace Minter, who at the time was a local town pimp and petty dope peddler that Snookey would use as an important marijuana and heroin connect between South Carolina and Georgia's low country communities.

There was a strong and immediate attraction between the two, which developed into a full-fledged love affair spanning eleven years of bittersweet interaction, with Snookey Lake traveling back and forth between states to visit his illegitimate family when away from his wife and children down in New Orleans. He only referred to himself as Maureen's "friend" when in the company of mutual friends or family and demanded that his girlfriend do the same. But once his Georgia-born mistress became pregnant with their third child, Snookey became less loving and more distant, while Maureen's behavior was the polar opposite, being increasingly possessive and insecure and often sparking heated arguments between the couple.

Eventually Marion Lake left Maureen for good after one particularly violent row.

While Snookey Lake would return to his wife Melissa and their twins, Dawn and Shawn, Maureen would bear a second son, whom she'd call Alonzo, yet still loving the man who'd left her with three children, a cocaine addiction, and a broken heart that never completely mended afterwards.

"I got a shitload o' work to do today for the job, so I'm gonna need you to watch the boys for me for 'bout three or four hours. I'm a li'l behind on some paperwork that my boss needs when he gets back next week, so while he's away on vacation, I wanna catch up on it."

Whiskey waltzed over to the fridge and bent low into the open door amidst the frosty mist billowing out. He eyed the neatly stacked rows of foodstuffs for a beer. "A'ight, man, whatever. You just hurry up 'cause I got places to go and peoples to see, so bring yo' butt back here ASAP," he said jokingly, plucking a cold bottle of Corona from between a container of leftover meatloaf and fruit punch.

"Nigga, please," she retorted with a sly grin, while preparing the plates with steaming-hot breakfast chow. "Ron, Kelly, Barry, get off that game an' wash y'all's hands for breakfast."

"A'ight, Mama, we comin'!" Ron yelled. He dropped the game controller and bolted toward the bathroom door, and his two brothers quickly followed him.

Whiskey helped his sister set the dining room table for breakfast. Homemade grits laden in butter sat steaming beside thick slabs of country bacon and stacks of buck-wheat pancakes slathered in maple syrup.

The mouth-watering aroma brought the three boys racing from the bathroom and into their awaiting seats with freshly washed hands, which their dutiful mother stopped briefly to inspect before continuing on with her morning meal preparation.

Tasha was a wonderful cook, a skill she'd learned from years of experience as a teen whose mother seemed to prefer all-night parties to responsible parenting. She'd graduated from peanut butter and jelly sandwiches to full-course turkey dinners on Thanksgiving and had seen to it that neither she nor her younger brothers ever went hungry. It got to a point that even when their mother was sober or at home long enough to attempt cooking, her bland dishes were left mostly untouched in favor of Tasha's more savory meals, which she herself greedily devoured.

After finishing up at the dinner table, Tasha left her sons behind eating heartily as she returned to the kitchen to prepare her own plate of Southern-style victuals. She then spotted a plain white envelope lying on the green marble tile of the kitchen countertop.

"Didn't I ask you to stop bringin' dis shit in here for me?" Tasha flashed the wad of cash she'd just removed from the envelope. "I don't need it, and I don't want it, okay?"

"That's over a thousand dollars right there. Don't tell me dat you don't need it 'cause I know better." Whiskey took a quick swallow of beer and belched loudly as he leaned up against the kitchen wall and faced his big sister.

"Look here, li'l boy, don't come in here talkin' that ol' bullshit to me, a'ight? You gonna respect me, and you damn sho' gonna respect my house. I work for a livin', an' don't you forget it! Every two weeks I bring home a nice paycheck that lets me take care of me an' my kids, so I don't need any of your dope money to take care of my needs. Now just take ya li'l twelve hundred dollars back, 'cause we ain't hardly hurtin' for nothin'!"

"A'ight, a'ight, my bad, sis. You know I would never disrespect you or your house. I just wanna do my part to kinda help out some 'round here an' show my appreciation for everything you've done an' still continue to do, dat's all." Whiskey looked up at Tasha sheepishly. "You're always workin' so hard, and ever since Ma got locked up two years ago, you been workin' harder than ever. So I just wanna do a li'l somethin' for you an' my nephews 'cause dey daddies don't do shit for 'em no way."

Whiskey finished the bottle of Corona and placed it gently into the kitchen garbage pail and folded his well-muscled arms across his broad chest as he awaited a response from his sister, who stared at him in front of the refrigerator, hands akimbo on her wide hips.

"First of all, Ma was a deadbeat parent way before she got hooked on crack and decided to rob that 7-Eleven. She didn't do shit for none of us, an' you know this. An', yes, the fathers of my boys ain't worth shit either. Both of 'em ain't nothin' but sperm donors. I know this better than anybody, but that's my problem, not yours. I appreciate your concern, but mind your business. I got this. An' as for you helpin' out around here, you my brother, you ain't gotta do nothing but take out the trash, keep my car runnin' good, and babysit every now an' then, and that's all. You're my little brother, not my man, so I don't expect for you to take care of me. But I do wish that you'll leave all o' dem li'l hoodlum-ass friends you hang around alone, 'cause I don't want you gettin' yourself caught up like our mama or our criminal-ass daddy, Snookey."

"Ain't nobody gonna get in trouble, you trippin'. An' our father got snitched on by our cousin Rae-Kwon an' dem. If it hadn't been for his bitch ass, our pops would be out right now."

"Don't even go there with me, boy. Snookey left us high an' dry a long time ago, an' he even got our sister Dawn killed, fuckin' with that hustlin' lifestyle. What kinda role model dad is that? And don't you dare blame

Rae-Kwon for Snookey's arrest. Hell, I woulda helped bring him down myself, 'cause he was nothin' but a cancer to this whole community. His own wife left his tired ass, and Shawn ain't been right since Dawn was killed. He's the reason our mama got strung out on that shit. Fuck Snookey Lake wit' a sick dick, an' I mean that shit!"

"A'ight, sis, calm down. I'm sorry I brought dat shit up. My bad." Whiskey gently came over and planted a kiss on his sister's rosy cheek before returning to the fridge to fish around for another bottle of beer.

He found one, closed the door, popped the top on the cold brew and took a deep swallow. "I'm always gonna be on yo' side, no matter what, even though I don't fully agree with you on everything you say, just like I know you don't agree with me all da time. But dat's life, an' it's all good. I just want you to know how much I love you, sis, dat's all."

"Yeah, yeah, I guess you a'ight." Tasha smiled as she embraced her younger sibling, warmly kissing him on his forehead as they hugged. Tasha felt more of a maternal bond with Whiskey than that of an older sister. After all, it was she who had changed his dirty diapers and burped him when their mother was away, which was most of the time.

After the brief expression of love and sentimental feelings between the siblings, Whiskey backed away and emptied the Corona bottle of its golden contents in one huge gulp, belched out loudly, and tossed the empty bottle in the trash.

"A'ight, Tasha, go ahead an' do what you gotta do 'cause I gotta holla at Alonzo at seven o'clock out Badlands Manor an' shit. So you gotta hurry back, okay?"

Tasha sighed with disgust at the mention of her youngest brother.

Alonzo Battle was by far the most volatile of the three siblings, causing mischief throughout his tender twenty years. He'd been arrested multiple times since the age of fourteen, the latest arrest landing him in the Peola county jail for a year and a half for violating his parole. He strongly resembled both Snookey Lake and his late half-sister Dawn, and also possessed their hair-trigger temper.

Tasha had kicked Alonzo out of her home twice in the past for repeated infractions. She had to constantly warn him about smoking marijuana in the apartment while her boys were present, or packages of drugs stashed in closets and dresser drawers, not to mention guns and the unopened boxes of ammunition that went with them. Alonzo also, unlike Whiskey, could be belligerent and rude to his older sister, especially when he'd been drinking.

"So what's his li'l no-mannered ass doin' with himself now?"

Whiskey shook his head, trying to think of a way to skip the subject of Alonzo's chronic life of crime, which had become a tired source of debate between them over the years. "C'mon, Tasha, you know Alonzo gonna do what he do. Ain't no changin' dat cat. But, hey, he gotta live his life for himself, not us."

"Yeah, you're absolutely right. I just hope that he gets himself together one of these days, 'cause I ain't ready to bury him just yet."

Whiskey nodded in agreement, though he wished deep down inside that his two siblings could finally let bygones be bygones and come together as a family again.

* * *

As soon as Tasha returned home, she arrived to a well-vacuumed, neatly arranged home that smelled of fragrant Khush incense. Her three young boys were all fast asleep in their beds, snoring lightly. Tasha apologized to her brother for arriving home so late.

Whiskey shrugged it off, though, because he felt that babysitting was the least he could do for a sister who'd done so much for him. Besides, he greatly enjoyed spending time with his rambunctious little nephews whenever he could.

Twenty-year-old Alonzo Battle sold illegal narcotics such as cocaine, heroin, ecstasy and crystal meth out of his three-bedroom apartment he shared with his girlfriend and her two-year-old son out in Badlands Manor. He also worked as a bouncer at the 95 South nightclub in West Peola, where he got most of his drug clientele, which many times included undercover cops. On weekends, he and Whiskey would hook up at the club or at one of North Peola's sports bars to flirt with the sexy waitresses, watch the big games, or simply talk business.

Alonzo usually bounced on Friday and Saturday nights, and occasionally during the weekdays whenever he provided security for personal events like bachelor parties, card parties, or pool parties. But, on this particular evening, he'd phoned his brother from the famed restaurant, Big Mama's Kitchen, out in West Peola.

Big Mama's was hands down Peola's premier eatery. Located in the posh Pemmican County of the city's elite West Side, the beloved restaurant had been serving the residents of Peola and the surrounding area with fine

Southern cuisine since 1922. Everybody who was anybody dined there, and many locals boasted that it was
the single best five-star restaurant in the entire state of
Georgia. On weekends there was live music, jazz and
R&B performances on Saturdays, and on Sundays, the
soul-stirring renditions of the various local gospel
groups, their Southern Baptist spirituals bringing a bit of
church to the patrons as they dined.

Of the three siblings, the tall, sturdy Alonzo physically
resembled Snookey the most, with similar handsome facial features and dark, curly hair. In fact, he was the spitting image of his father. He wore his silky locks in long
braids that hung loosely down his broad back and wide
shoulders. Like many ex-cons, he boasted a post-prison
physique, which was magnificently buff and adorned
with homemade tattoos.

Rocking an army-green South Pole cotton tee, a pair of
baggy Rocawear denim shorts, a sparkling 24-carat
white gold herringbone chain with a brilliant diamond-
cluttered Jesus charm, he was covered with the scent of
weed and Issey Miyake.

And from the look of his reddened eyes, he was well
beyond just a simple buzz.

As he embraced his older brother, his breath screamed
of one too many Hennessy and Coke.

"'S up wit' cha, big brotha?" Alonzo said, smiling
broadly through his diamond-studded grills. "Whatcha
been up to, nigga?"

"Just tryin' to maintain out dis bitch, dat's all. What
'bout you?" Whiskey said, hugging his baby brother
tightly against his chest.

"Bouncin', hustlin', fuckin' bad bitches, you know

how we do it down in da South Side. Da blocks been kinda hot lately since bitch-ass O'Malley done cracked down on da coke shipments out on da Gosa Harbor, so cats ain't been pumpin' dat 'girl' like dey used to, ya know. But, hey, real niggas know how ta switch dey game up in order ta get dat work regardless, feel me?"

Whiskey nodded in agreement and took up a menu, while a cute waitress stood patiently in the background. "Sup wit' Paul Ballard an' shit?" Whiskey asked, briefly peering over the leather-bound menu in his hands.

"You askin' me? Shit, dat's yo' boy. I should be askin' you what's up. He got shit locked down on da South Side. Been dat way since ninety-four, you know dat ya-self, dawg."

"No doubt." Whiskey ordered a pitcher of Corona Extra and a forty-dollar fisherman's platter.

After Alonzo wolfed down every bit of his expensive meal, he eased back in his seat, wiped his greasy mouth with a cotton handkerchief, and ordered yet another glass of Hennessy and Coke, flirting with the blushing waitress the whole time. "I ain't really hollered at too many cats since I got outta da pen a while back, you know, but you know Paul got juice like a mufucka out on dese country-ass streets and dirt roads 'round here. So everybody know dat half-white mufucka got shit on lock. Shit, he even got da chief o' police kissin' his ass."

Alonzo flirted even more when the attractive waitress returned with both of their orders. She smiled bashfully and returned to her duties as the drunken young hustler spewed catcalls and wolf whistles her way.

"Yeah, he got shit on lock wit' da hustlin', but I done

heard he stepped his game up by fuckin' wit' da po-po, similar to what you doin'."

"Well, da old sayin' goes, if ya can't beat 'em, join 'em. I guess dat's what da boys in blue is doin' now, 'cause you got a coupla crooked-ass cops, crackas, and niggas alike makin' plenty money, rubbin' elbows wit' us hot boys, ya know?"

"Paul been locked up wit' me too for 'bout four months befo' he got out. He said he been in contact wit' Snookey through some Black Gangster Disciples in Akron. He told me our daddy gon' be transferred to Akron in September of this year. Once dat happens, shit gon' be pumpin' like old times back on da streets."

"Paul oughta know 'cause he done been locked down way longer than me, an' he got connections in da pen dat reach all over da whole country."

"Dat's all gravy an' everything, but I believe shit when I see it for myself an' not befo'." Whiskey sighed as he poured himself a tall glass of brew. "I done talked to Paul myself 'bout his dealins' wit' da po-po, but da part 'bout him doin' bidness wit' Snookey, I still gotta see for myself."

Alonzo shrugged off his brother's skepticism as he sipped on his sixth round of Henny and Coke. "Yeah, Paul got it goin' on. He had a nice li'l bit o' money comin' to 'im back when we was both locked up down in Akron too. He was pretty well connected wit' da gangs inside, like da Geechee-Gullah Nation and da Black Guerilla Family. He sold lotsa weed and more than a li'l bit o' powda. He even slung some smack whenever he could get it from da Latino cats."

"I know, 'cause I helped 'im sell a lot o' da dope myself," Whiskey said.

"Yep. When he graduated high school, he musta served dope to the whole fuckin' senior class, teachers included."

Whiskey nodded. "Yeah, him and David Ambrosia's brother, Lee. They was pumpin' a whole lotta weight through school back in da day, an' when Dawn, Shawn, and Rae-Kwon came to Caymon High and hooked up wit' 'im, it was on an' poppin' for real after that."

"But crackhead-ass Jason Dombrowski fucked everything up when he snitched on niggas after O'Malley arrested his dumb ass for breakin' into his house, tryin' to boost shit." Alonzo paused to glance lustfully at the plump backside of a passing waitress as she bent over to retrieve a crumpled ten-dollar tip she'd just dropped.

"But back to da matter, when I was in da pen, I used to fuck wit' a whole lotta Jamaican niggas. Now I know back in da day, when da South Peola homies was beefin' wit' dem dreads in Badlands Manor and Geneva Projects, shit was ugly 'tween us an' dem boys. But I got to know dat dem dreads ain't so bad in da joint. As a matter o' fact, I did bidness wit' dis one cat from Kingston name Richard Olson, but cats in da pen called 'im Deadeye Dick 'cause he lost his right eye back in da day in a knife fight as a teenager in Kingston. He was da head o' da Trenchtown Posse up in Akron, and dey controlled fifty percent of all da dope comin' in da pen, while da 'eses' and skinheads split da rest. While I was locked up, this dude became a fuckin' legend up in da pen. Niggas inside was sayin' ain't nobody made da type o' paper nor had da juice like Deadeye since our cousin Rae-Kwon and dat ol' Jewish pimp, Lionel Kurtz, was doin' it big back in da eighties. I know for damn sho I musta pulled in over five grand a week when I was pumpin' for 'im while we were both inside a while back. He had da C.O.'s on lock. Da warden and even cops on da outside was workin' for 'im.

"He bought the Lion's Den nightclub after Big Gabby got sent to da pen, and he done opened up three more nightclubs. Plus, he got a big recordin' studio in North Peola where wannabe rappers an' amateur singers go to audition and lay down tracks while sellin' dope outta dem joints da whole damn time on da low.

"Right befo' I got outta da pen, some hatin'-ass niggas got wit' some dudes on da outside who was beefin' wit' da Trenchtown Posse, and befo' ya know it, da feds had a sting operation dat shut da whole program da fuck down. 'Round 'bout twenty-five prison guards got convicted on federal drug charges. Dat included da warden too. Cats wit' as little as two years left got hit wit' ten mo' years for being part o' da ring. I was real lucky, 'cause I'd stopped sellin' shit six months befo', 'cause I got wit' dese Muslim dudes an' called myself 'goin' righteous' for a hot minute. Turns out dat Allah musta saved my black ass for sho', 'cause if it wasn't for me reppin' Islam, I woulda gotten caught up wit' da rest o' dem po' bastards. Deadeye was da ringleader o' da whole thing, so da feds hit him wit' da kingpin statute, and a federal jury up in Atlanta found him guilty on all counts, from drug trafficking and murder to blackmail and extortion. He was nailed wit' a hunit an' ten years in federal prison. I don't know where he's at now. All I know is dat he's locked down in supermax. Cats say Deadeye is somethin' like one hundred feet underground all alone in a cell by himself, watched by closed-circuit cameras, and armed guards are his only human contact. He never sees daylight, and no one can call, visit, or write him—He's fucked for life."

The cute waitress came back with Whiskey's pitcher of beer and Alonzo's Henny and Coke, while a baby-faced waiter, no older than eighteen, gently placed the steaming fisherman's platter in front of Whiskey.

Alonzo hastily drank down the potent, syrupy elixir, grimacing as the warm rush of Hennessy opened like wings in his chest. "Niggas was gettin' on da map like a mufucka when dat one-eyed cat was bossin' up. Dude put hustlas on, rap niggas on, fly-ass bitches on. *Sheeet*, nigga, even da po-po got on. Nigga, my man brung a lot o' paper to a whole lotta folks, inside da joint an' out. I know for damn sho I was one, so da hood gotta show son some love.'

Whiskey nodded, biting into a succulent piece of baked salmon then shrugged his shoulders, making eye contact with his younger brother on the opposite side of the dinner table.

The waitress again approached the pair as they sat conversing in the back of the restaurant in the secluded VIP section of the entertainment-themed eatery that was their usual dining spot. "May I bring y'all anything else, gentlemen?" the blushing girl asked, presenting a bright, dimpled smile.

The boys, now engrossed in hustle talk, waved her away politely and continued on with business.

"Dat's all good, an' I feel you on my man's hustle an' everything, but what da fuck he gotta do wit' yo' hustle?

A'ight, bet, Peola's police chief, O'Malley, been runnin' five-O round dese parts for years. Since our daddy been locked up, niggas ain't been gettin' dey money right. Dat's been for a minute now, so niggas from Peola, and Savannah hustlas too, done hooked up wit' Cackalacky niggas out in Beaufort County, an' we been bringin' dope from New York and Miami to Hilton Head Airport. Snookey and da Fuskie Krew brings da shit on a boat to Daufuskie Island, where dudes load 'em and start drivin' packages back to da stash trailer down on Haig's Point ta weigh an' bag up, proper like. Snookey's at Bloody Point prison puttin' in work an' makin' moves from inside an' outside. Dat's been gettin' fuckas rich. Niggas been makin' so much money, dat now da police wanna get in da game?" Whiskey asked.

Alonzo took a swig of his drink. "Now some o' dem boys in blue want money just like cats in da game, an' dey approached us wit' a deal. Dey watch our backs, and we'll watch dey's, so I'd say 'bout a hundred cops, black an' white, 'specially white boys, though, is makin' sho dat da coke money comin' in from Daufuskie is greasin' all o' our palms 'cause Daufuskie coke is servin' da whole Souf Cack and Georgia low country. You know how much money dat is, Whiskey? *Sheeet*, nigga, we bring in somethin' like five million dollars a year or more. I really don't know for sho, but I do know dat it was four million plus. Anyway, we got one small problem," Alonzo said in a thick Gullah accent. "We need you ta get rid o' Mickey O'Malley's bitch ass 'cause jus' as ol' bitch-ass Rossum, former New Orleans' police chief, had set him up in top-cop status here in Peola, he was invited to spend two months on Daufuskie Island to help train and prepare the Daufuskie police to handle the growing drug trafficking they'd faced for da past three years. Now you know dem gutta-ass niggas out here ain't gonna let dat fat-ass Irish mufucka fuck dey money up no longer."

Whiskey nodded and continued eating his seafood meal.

"So what's up? You down, or what?" Alonzo reached across the table and grasped the half-filled pitcher of Miller Genuine Draft to pour himself a glass of the golden brew. "Da cops I'm workin' wit' is willin' to give you fifty grand for da hit. O'Malley is currently rentin' out a townhouse on Melrose Plantation. I can have his whereabouts to you in a day or two, a'ight?"

Whiskey stared down into his half-eaten meal and rubbed his tired eyes slowly, contemplating this latest offer of murder-for-hire. "Alonzo, I dunno 'bout dis one here, playa. If I do take yo' cop buddies up on dey offer, I'm-a get a coupla li'l young cats I know to do da hit, and then I'll pay dem afterwards. Don't worry, dese youngsters is some junkyard dawgs when it comes to pushin' niggas' wigs back, 'specially if you payin' 'em for it an' whatnot."

"Good, man. Dat's da deal, pimpin'. Anyway, on a different subject, how's Tasha and da boys doin'?"

"She doin' good. Da boys, dey a'ight too. She just stay worryin' and thinkin' 'bout yo black ass most o' da time. Dat's 'bout it."

"I dunno what fo'. She treated a nigga like a stepchild when I was stayin' dere an' shit."

"Anyway, I been helpin' David at the studio, layin' down tracks for his fiancée Godiva, for her upcomin' album this winter."

"You mean, *the* Godiva? Ambrosia's 'bout ta wife that fine-ass thang? Dat's one lucky-ass mufuckin' dude."

"Luck ain't got shit ta do wit' it, baby boy. David got game, dat's all, an' da good sense to know a good bidness move when he sees one."

"So you think she'll win da *Pop Star* competition? 'Cause Gina Madison can blow just as well as Godiva, if not better."

Whiskey gave his brother a quick smirk as he popped a piece of grilled shrimp into his mouth.

"A'ight, I know Godiva's a sexy dime an' all, an' she got pipes like a sista, but I dunno if dat lily-white girl got what it takes to knock off a diva like Gina Madison, 'cause last week my girl was watchin' da shit on TV an' she said dey both sung a half-hour's worth of Anita Baker's songs, an' Madison sounded much betta than da white girl. An' my girl watch dat show every Thursday religiously."

"Everybody's entitled to dey own opinion, Alonzo, your girl included, but it's no way America is gonna let another black singer win a major singing competition. Shit, Fantasia already done won it all on *American Idol* just last year. Plus, Godiva is younger, prettier, and she got a mo' bubbly personality than Gina Madison. And don't ever forget the number one kicker—she's white! She's a young, blond-haired, blue-eyed dime piece wit' a bubble butt like a sista and, like you even said, the voice to match. Now Madison can sing her ass off, I know, but she's twenty-nine, short, overweight, dusty black and ugly. I love my black women, just like you, but hey, I'm also one ta keep it real. She ain't got a snowball's chance in hell to win *Pop Star* over Godiva."

"Damn, nigga! You pumpin' dat white bitch up a whole lot, ain't ya, bro? Shit, you reppin' dat ho like you dickin' her down or somethin'—is you? *Sheeet*, inquirin' minds wanna know," Alonzo said.

"Naw, dawg, I don't mix bidness wit' pleasure, you know dat. Besides, David's my man. I'd never violate homie like dat."

"Yeah, okay. I betcha if dat broad offer up da ass, you ain't gonna turn it down, an' ya ain't gonna think twice 'bout ya boy David. Tell me I'm wrong."

Whiskey poured himself a glass of cold beer after downing the first one and grinned softly. "She is a keeper for damn sho, I agree wit' ya on dat, my man. An' if she wasn't David's girl, yeah, I'd fuck her." He swallowed a mouthful of the golden ale.

"Yeah, don't lie to me. I'm yo' li'l brotha, nigga. I know dat befo' too long you gon' be screwin' Godiva right under David's nose. Watch what I tell you."

Whiskey pushed his half-eaten meal to the side and waved the pretty waitress over to their table. "Check please, gorgeous." Then he tipped her a fifty and winked at her, to which she responded with a bashful smile.

Chapter 4

"Get This Money Right"

"Peola's famous top cop, Police Chief Mickey O'Malley vows to assist Daufuskie Island's fledgling police force with training and recruiting to crack down on the sea island's rising drug trade, which has made it a haven for both local and out-of-state drug traffickers. O'Malley's success as a police chief is well documented in Bryan, Chatham, Effingham, and Peola Counties, where his hard-edged, highly unorthodox style of policing has brought both praise and criticism his way.

"The controversial police chief stated, 'Criminals are criminals. It doesn't matter whether they're punk kids vandalizing churches with spray paint or millionaire drug cartels flying coke into our country from Colombia. They're all scum to me, and their crimes can't be tolerated for any reason. I live to lock these animals up and see to it that they're taken off the streets for a helluva long time, 'cause I don't want 'em in my town, my state, my region, or in my country, period.' "

Whiskey changed the remote from local Channel 11 to ESPN after the report on Mickey O'Malley's Sea Island drug war came to a close. It was painfully obvious that O'Malley was just as obsessed with ridding Daufuskie of dope-peddling riffraff as he had been with his native Peola. Even more ironic was Channel 11's commercial featuring the upcoming televised *Pop Star* grand finale pitting the sexy, well-liked blonde against her equally popular opponent.

Godiva was America's latest sweetheart, having joined Ciara and Ludacris on stage during a sold-out concert at the Georgia Dome, where she was greeted by a five-minute round of thunderous applause for her rendition of Ciara's hit song, "Oh." She was even invited to the Governor's Mansion in Atlanta.

Whiskey marveled at the dimensions of the girl's curves, which rivaled the thickest sista. He knew that she was Rae-Kwon's baby mama and currently the fiancée of his best friend, but from the eyes she would give him and the way she would put an extra wiggle in her walk each time he'd show up at the studio, he knew it was but a matter of time before he'd hit that phat white ass.

As he channel-surfed he could think of little else than how he'd go about murdering the chief of police. It could be perhaps his most challenging hit yet. He himself often paid underlings to take care of his murder-for-hire gigs when he either couldn't do it himself or felt that the job was too lightweight for him to consider carrying out himself. Those were usually small-time jobs—a few hundred dollars here, a kilo of coke there—but this was a big-time operation that needed time and patience to be taken care of properly, not to mention the resources.

O'Malley was a hater of drug dealers, and somewhat of a racist, having been born and bred up North in racially prejudiced Boston. He had totally wiped out illegal drug traffic throughout Peola altogether shortly after Snookey Lake and his ecstasy ring was brought to justice back in 1994. Only David Ambrosia's Bad Boyz II Syndicate made moves on the street, and that was because he had a good working relationship with O'Malley and several other high-ranking Peola police officers. Niggas on the streets of South Peola had wanted to rid themselves of the gung ho Irishman for well over a decade now. Yet, with Chief O'Malley's popularity and political power among the town's movers and shakers, it was a pipe dream at best.

Ever since Daufuskie Island was discovered to be more than simply another sunny Sea Island resort, O'Malley was stepping on the toes of much more organized and vengeful traffickers than before, including the seemingly straight-laced Ambrosia. There were corrupt cops and other equally unethical lawmakers on the take, unbeknownst to him, who were not about to let Peola's 2004 Man of the Year ruin a good thing. He was marked for death, and didn't even know it.

It was well into the evening when the mid-sized yacht, *Island Skipper*, pulled up to the dock at Daufuskie's Haig Point landing. The raucous humming chorus of crickets and cicadas filled the air as Whiskey and the other passengers left the cabin of the boat and stepped out onto the worn, wooden planks of the dock. Awaiting them was a cheesy, green-and-white tour mobile, which doubled as a Metro Bus of sorts for island residents after normal business hours.

The driver, an old black man with a curly, white beard and receding hair around his bald pate, kept the dozen or so passengers laughing at lame jokes and engrossed in conversation on everything from deviled crab ingredients to President Bush's unpopular war in Iraq .

When he'd dropped off the last old geezer at the Melrose Plantation, he drove along the lonely dirt road for over twenty minutes in silence before he decided to address the young man sitting three rows behind to his rear, staring out of the window in deep thought.

"How you doin' today, young man?"

"I'm a'ight. How 'bout yaself?"

"Oh, I'm blessed by da best. At sixty-four years old, I just thank da good Lord fa health and strength."

"No doubt. But where can I go ta get a drink and maybe see some cuties?"

The old driver cackled through yellowed, rotted teeth. "Well, sir, I'll tell ya what. 'Round here you got da Haig's Point Inn. Dey sells a lot o' beer and wine, 'specially a coupla bottle wines made right chere on da island by us Fuskie folks. Then ya got Melrose Bar and Grill where you can get some hard liquor, plus a nice meal. They gots some jazz on some nights and country western on some nights. You can dance a li'l bit if ya wanna, but ain't no titty bars 'round here, if dat's what ya talkin' 'bout. Dese rich crackas ain't havin' no titty bars 'round here. Dey got too much tourist dollars ta make. Image, ya know? Now if ya go back to da mainland, I know ya can find mo' titty bars than a li'l bit."

Whiskey said from the back of the tour bus, "Damn!

Ain't nuttin' a nigga can do down here but play golf and go crabbin', huh?"

"You gotta realize, young man, this island is for two kinds o' people—old black folk and rich, middle-aged white folk. Now you got black folk yo' age livin' on da island here an' there, but dey up to no good, mostly sellin' dat dope ta dem rich whiteys down on Bloody Point Plantation, Melrose and Haig's Point Plantation. But it done got so bad dat dey done gone an' brung a big city police from Georgia ta get rid o' all dis goddamn dope from 'round here, 'cause dese li'l bicycle-ridin' po-po here on Fuskie can't do nuttin' wit' dem gun-totin' niggas from down in Webb Place and Dunn Gardens."

"Hmm, dat's a trip, 'cause I'm stayin' wit' one o' my peeps out in Webb Place for a few days. Who knows, maybe I'll fuck around an' play a li'l bit o' golf myself."

Upon hearing from his young passenger that the drug-ridden trailer park was his destination, he wrinkled his already furrowed brow even more in deep thought as he drove along the scenic greenery of sprawling golf courses and exquisitely manicured plantation lawns surrounding majestic-looking Southern homes, dusk slowly falling on the sleepy sea island.

"Is dat a'ight wit' you?" Whiskey asked somewhat sarcastically, sensing the old man's sudden discomfort.

The eyes of the driver met Whiskey's from the rear-view mirror above. "Well, to tell ya da truth, I ain't gonna drive up in Webb Place fa nobody, not even my own chillen an' dem. You gon' have ta get out here on Silver-dew Drive, young man. I's real sorry 'bout dis, but dat's how it's gotta be fa now, 'cause I's off-duty."

Whiskey tossed a small duffle bag across his broad

shoulder as he made his way off the tour bus and onto the gravel-lined sidewalk below.

It was but a short twenty-minute walk through a winding footpath in an overgrown palmetto-dotted thicket before reaching the entrance of Webb Place. Nappy-haired little Gullah girls played hopscotch and jumped double Dutch among the run-down mobile homes as bare-chested teen boys threw a weather-beaten football back and forth along the dusty backroad of the heavily populated trailer park.

Whiskey walked up the wooden steps of an old eggshell-white doublewide and knocked several times on the door.

A tall, handsome boy with sharp facial features and dark, satin-like skin opened the door and immediately embraced him with a broad smile and hearty laughter, while welcoming him into the living room.

"My nigga! 'S up witcha, boy?" Theo offered Whiskey the freshly rolled blunt he'd been puffing on.

"Ain't shit, shawty. Still pimpin', steady hustlin', stayin' trill wit' it, you know." Whiskey dragged deeply on the smoldering Dutch.

"My nigga, tryin' ta be like me an' shit. C'mon, lemme take you to ya room, so you can getcha self comfy-like."

Theo took a hold of Whiskey's duffle bag and proceeded down the long, carpeted hallway toward the room at the rear of the trailer. The room was mid-sized with an old cobweb-covered bureau dresser against a crayon-marked wall. A small electric lamp with a Power Ranger print lampshade sat upon the top of the dresser, illuminating the kiddie room in a soft yellow glow.

"You must be a fool for mufuckin' Power Rangers, huh?" Whiskey looked around at the Power Rangers posters, throw rugs, and action figures that adorned the entire area.

"Naw. What had happened was, I used ta fuck dis ho back in da day who had a li'l five-year-old—Da pussy was good. I moved da bitch and her son up in da crib, right? Well, da li'l nigga was a fiend fa Power Rangers, right, so I figured dat I'd hook his ass up wit' a Power Ranger-themed room an' shit, right. Man, dat li'l knucklehead loved dis shit. Too bad his mama had ta get caught cheatin' on me wit' da li'l nigga's daddy, so I kicked her hoin' ass up outta here. I just ain't never get around ta re-decoratin' dis mufucka, dat's all."

Whiskey passed the blunt back to Theo after coughing loudly for several seconds after his last toke.

"Yeah! Dat's dat purple haze, boy. Whatcha know 'bout dat?" Theo took the strong-smelling weed-filled cigar from his guest's outstretched hand.

"Oh fuck, yeah, dat's da shit right dere. I know you got big clientele off dis smoke right here, don't cha?" Whiskey asked, unpacking his belongings on the bed.

"What? Does barnyard hog like slop? *Sheeet*, nigga, I gotta re-up 'bout every three or fo' days, no bullshit."

Just then a cute, freckled-faced, fair-skinned girl in her early twenties walked past the open door of the room and sashayed down the hall toward the living room. Then she entered the kitchen and disappeared from view.

"You coulda shut da fuckin' do', ya know, li'l high-yella heifa!" Theo moved out into the hallway to close the door of the adjacent room from where the music of Three 6 Mafia blared loudly out into the darkened hallway.

"Who's dat, Theo?" Whiskey asked, brimming with sexual interest.

"Oh, dat li'l chickenhead? Dat's my first cousin, Charmaine. Why? You tryin' ta spit some game at her?"

Whiskey smirked as he shot his Geechee friend a look of disbelief. "C'mon now, what do you think?"

"A'ight. Excuse me, pimpin'. *Sheeet*, pop ya mufuckin' collar then, playa-playa."

"She got a man?"

"She used to, but he went off to Parris Island to enlist in da Marine Corps two years ago. Now Bush got his black ass fightin' in Iraq ." Theo passed the blunt back to Whiskey as they both sat on the bed.

"How old is she?"

"She just turned twenty-two in June."

"Damn! She's just two years younger than me. Dat's a'ight. She a bad mufucka, I know dat much. She got chillen?" Whiskey finished off the last of the blunt before smashing it down into a nearby ashtray, and the last thin wisp of smoke dissipated into the air.

"Naw, she ain't got no chillen, nigga. She ain't even never been pregnant, dawg! She know betta. *Sheet*, Charmaine goin' ta college at Savannah State. She just here visitin' for da summer, dat's all."

Whiskey stroked his neatly trimmed goatee, nodding his head thoughtfully. The cutie was both sexy and smart all at the same time. Plus, she didn't have any little snot-nosed brats hanging around. It seemed to him that she was ripe for the picking.

"A'ight, c'mon. Let's stop sittin' 'round here chattin' like a couple o' old-ass bitches an' whatnot an' go out on da back porch wit' her, if you tryin' ta put ya bid in, 'cause dat's where she likes ta chill out at all da time."

"True, true. A'ight, lemme get a dub o' dat haze up off you. Gimme da fattest bag you got on you." Whiskey, attempted to hand his host a crisp twenty-dollar bill from a thick rubber band-wrapped wad of cash he took from the right pocket of his baggy jean shorts.

"C'mon, Whiskey, wit' dat ol' bullshit, nigga. Take dis bag o' reefer an' git da fuck on. You know I don't charge my peeps fa nuttin'. Now go 'head an' enjoy yaself 'cause I'm 'bout ta head to Benning's Point. I gotta drop off some X pills to some crackas at da lighthouse. Dey s'pose ta be havin' some late-night beach party or somethin'. I'm one o' da few black mufuckas dey invited. Shit, I'm-a go too. Ya never know, I might get a coupla dem white bitches ta suck on dis wood, ya know what I mean?"

"Well, if you servin' up dat X, you know fa sho da very least you gonna get is sloppy deep-throat action from dem white hoes. You know dey good fa givin' dat brain, but I need fa you ta bring me a small container o' kerosene or gas, a'ight?"

"What da fuck you gon' be needin' shit like dat for?"

"Nigga, don't worry 'bout it. Just make it happen, cap'n, a'ight?"

Theo nonchalantly flipped him off as he snatched a cluster of keys from the top of the dresser. "Whatever, dawg. I'll bring dat shit back on da rebound 'cause I'm on my way out da do'. Holla atcha a li'l while later."

Whiskey smiled, clasped hands with Theo in a brotherly show of affection, and followed his host to the front door. There they briefly engaged in further small talk before they both went their separate ways. Whiskey walked back down the hall to the room at the end and entered again to finish unpacking.

After that and a hot shower he emerged from the room rocking a pair of basketball shorts and a Dwayne Wade, Miami Heat jersey. His dark, silky hair was freshly braided and draped down his thick neck, and ended in miniature red-and-white dice at the tips. He briefly touched up his mustache and goatee in the partially broken mirror in the hall bathroom, afterwards putting down the electric shaver and picking up a radiant platinum necklace that shimmered with polished brilliance against the black knit nylon of the jersey.

He smiled with satisfaction at the well-groomed image he beheld in the mirror before him. He blasted his open mouth with breath spray, smacked his lips, and applied a copious amount of Kenneth Cole's Reaction cologne all over his jersey before stepping out into the hallway and towards the living room.

Once there he turned toward the kitchen from which the delightfully melodious ballads of Alicia Keys filtered out from the screen door bordering the outdoor porch.

As he walked into the kitchen, he noticed a bottle of Armadale Vodka and a container of orange juice on the countertop and several empty glasses nearby. He helped himself to a glass and walked through the screen door and out onto the porch, where various moths, fireflies, and water beetles fluttered around a naked light bulb overhead.

Charmaine sat cross-legged in a huge, cushiony wicker

chair, sipping on a screwdriver and reading a copy of Sister Souljah's book, *The Coldest Winter Ever.*

Whiskey took in the beauty of the female he gazed upon and was immediately smitten. With a pair of lovely legs and bulging cleavage straining against the sheer fabric of her paisley-printed blouse, she slowly twitched her manicured toes within the dangling stiletto, stopping to look up from her novel to peer at the man who stood in the middle of the floor silently admiring her good looks.

Whiskey salivated as he realized that Charmaine was even more attractive than he'd originally thought. As her soft amber eyes met his, he smiled and moved slowly over to her, extending his hand in an informal greeting while the sexy vixen wrapped her full red lips around the thin straw.

He felt his wood stiffen within his boxers. "'S up witcha, shawty? My name's Peter, but my peeps all call me Whiskey, ya know. So my man Theo is ya cousin, huh?"

Charmaine placed her book face down in her lap and reached forward, putting her delicate hand into Whiskey's for a light handshake. "Hi ya doin'? My name's Charmaine. It's a pleasure meetin' you finally. Theo been talkin' 'bout you for da last two weeks, an' so it's finally good to put a face wit' a name. Yeah, Theo is my first cousin, unfortunately—Naw, I'm just playin'. I love that boy; he's my heart."

"I heard you go to Savannah State. What you takin' up?" Whiskey pulled up a chair next to hers.

"Well, I major in pediatrics and minor in child development studies. I also cheerlead during da football and basketball seasons."

"What! Shit! Now I know why you got such a tight-ass body an' shit."

"Thank you! I'm flattered. Our team leader puts a lot of physical demands on all of us, so we gotta keep it tight at all times." She raised her drink to her lips and took another sip.

"I know dat's right. Well, whatever it is dat you doin', keep it up 'cause it's damn sho workin'.'"

"Yeah, yeah, yeah. I betcha say that to all the girls, don't you?"

"Only if dey's fine as you."

"Um-hmm. See what I'm talkin' 'bout. You ain't nothin' but a ho, ain't cha? Probably got a bunch o' baby mamas from Fuskie to Peola, don't cha?"

"Naw, sorry, miss lady, but I ain't got no chillens or baby mamas neither, so get it right. You tryin' ta hit some o' dis?" Whiskey displayed an overstuffed bag of strong-smelling cannabis.

"Nope. I don't smoke dat shit, sorry. Don't you know that one blunt is worse for your health than smoking five cigarettes? Think about that next time you fire up a *J*, okay?"

Whiskey grinned while shaking his head. He swigged down the entire contents of the glass before stuffing the twenty-dollar bag of bud back into his pants pocket. "Hey, whatever's clever. To each her own. I ain't mad at cha. I just wanna get ta know ya betta, dat's all, pretty girl. How 'bout catchin' a movie an' a li'l somethin' to eat afterwards over on Hilton Head tonight?"

"I guess so . . . if you sure you ain't got nothin' else betta to do, like hangin' out wit' my cousin Theo."

"Theo's my man, fifty gran' an' all, but choosin' him

over you would be outrageous. Plus, he got things to do tonight anyway."

"Whatever you say, Peter. I refuse to call you *Whiskey*, 'cause yo' mama didn't name you dat, did she?"

"Girl, you got too much damn mouth, you know dat? But I like a woman wit' a li'l spunk to her. It gives me a challenge. But I'm gonna getcha mind right, watch."

Whiskey quickly went into the kitchen and came back with another round of screwdrivers for him and the young lady. He wanted to get into her pants before leaving Daufuskie by the end of the following week. Though she seemed like a tough cookie, those were, many times, the easiest to crack; it just took game.

After taking a long sip on her screwdriver, Charmaine took Whiskey's hand in hers. "Look, let's stop playin' games, okay. I'm turned on by you, and you are obviously turned on by me. We're both adults, consenting adults. Now just because I don't have any babies or fuck half the neighborhood doesn't mean that I'm some stuck-up, non-sexual being. I'm a very confident, self-assured gal, and at the moment, about as horny as a bitch in heat. So, while my cousin's away, let's take this opportunity to let nature take its course, okay?" Charmaine moved her slender fingers from Whiskey's hand to the swollen bulge in the front of his jeans and caressed his erection through the fabric of the denim.

Whiskey quickly and instinctively undid his belt, allowing his jeans to drop to the floor. His thick penis hung long and curved in Charmaine's smiling freckled face. Too drunk with lust to think of anything other than sexual release, Whiskey didn't seem to care that they were both on the front porch.

Charmaine hiked her skirt up while pulling her pink lace panties down around her thick, round thighs past her knees, calves and ankles. Then she pulled Whiskey toward her by his stiff member, guiding him into her moist, pink slit.

Whiskey pounded her in the missionary position.

Charmaine moaned out in ecstasy, "Ohhh, yes, fuck me, baby. Ohhh, God, yes. Fuck this pussy hard, baby, ohhh yeah," her shapely legs trembling with delight as she reached an orgasm.

Whiskey, who usually used condoms, pulled out his rod, glistening with Charmaine's vaginal secretions, and shot a thick stream of semen across her lower abdomen and pubic hair before collapsing back onto the large wicker chair where he'd previously sat, totally exhausted from the intense lovemaking.

Chapter 5

"For da Soldiers"

Daufuskie Island was an area that most people knew as a resort spot, but natives of the sea island knew that Daufuskie could prove deadly to any outsider who took the sleepy, down-home Gullah culture for granted. Several of Whiskey's homeboys had been members of the infamous Fuskie Krew gang, which was a part of the much larger Geechee-Gullah Nation, a low country version of Chicago's People and Folks Nations gangs.

One time, a crackhead from Hilton Head's Spanish Wells community got behind on his dope bill, and to add salt to the wound, he turned out to be a rat for the island's cops. This bit of street betrayal severely cut into Whiskey's drug profits, which had been quite profitable after he'd partnered up with the Fuskie Krew to distribute crack cocaine throughout the Beaufort County region.

* * *

It was August of 1999, and Whiskey had contacted Joi
Stevens, the crew's leader, and traveled down to Fuskie
to meet with the violent gang leader. Over a traditional
Gullah dinner of deviled crabs, fried oysters, and boiled
hominy grits, they discussed the details of the murder
that was to take place on Hilton Head.

When Reggie Dillon, a forty-six-year-old Beaufort
County sanitation worker, sat in his trash truck near
Hilton Head High, getting head from an underage girl,
Joi calmly walked up to the driver's side window and
pumped Dillon and his seventeen-year-old lover, Natalie
White, full of hollow-tip slugs before roaring away in a
black convertible BMWcoupe.

Joi was later caught and convicted of the double murder and sentenced to fifteen years at Daufuskie's Bloody
Point Beach prison. He had been ratted out by a senior
member of the crew, Marcus Finbarr, a.k.a. "Fin," who'd
been given a major deal by low country authorities to act
as an informant.

Whiskey knew of Fin's whereabouts on Hilton Head,
and he had already decided in his mind to avenge his
friend Joi. It had been six years since Joi Stevens had been
imprisoned for the murders of Reggie Dillon and Natalie
White. And over a dozen or more Fuskie Krew gang
members had been thrown in prison for various crimes
since then, greatly weakening the infrastructure of the
one-time powerful crew.

Fin was now living among Hilton Head's wealthy so-
cialites in the costly Sea Pines Plantation, a gated community, ferrying rich, retired geezers back and forth

between Hilton Head and Daufuskie on his modest-sized tour boat for $150-a-pop weekly. And he supplemented this lucrative income with the under-the-table monies given to him by the sheriff's office of Beaufort County for dropping dimes on his old crew and their activities. Fin usually worked Monday through Saturday, eleven AM to seven PM, and conducted no ferryboat tours on Sundays, which was when he normally refueled, repaired, and tidied up his small yacht for the coming workweek.

After a quick touch-up to her wavy hair, Charmaine got dressed in a hot pink Baby Phat cotton corset with a crystal logo and a matching pink cotton tennis skirt with pink leather go-go boots. The couple took Theo's second vehicle, an old gray Camry, to the docks at Haig Point.

Whiskey showered again and dressed in what he'd worn before his back-porch tryst with Charmaine. Only, this time he would be traveling with a black Desert Eagle 9 mm handgun with accompanying silencer, both of which he stuffed down into his jean shorts. Hopefully he'd be able to track down the snitch right after painting the town with Charmaine.

After paying the reduced round-trip fee for island natives, Whiskey and Charmaine boarded one of the several river taxis that lined the sides of the dock. Steaming along at about thirty-three knots through the dark, choppy waters of the Cooper River, the red-and-white striped tower of Harbour Town's famed lighthouse welcomed them to the posh shores of Hilton Head.

As the river taxi drew closer to the busy, brightly lit pier, Whiskey noticed the many tourists dining outside under the colorful canopies of the assorted eateries in the warmth of the summer night. Lively jazz and solemn blues blared out into the streets from a live quartet playing in the courtyard filled with couples mingling and dancing along the cobblestoned street.

Once their passenger boat docked at the pier, Whiskey and his companion exited the vessel and caught a cab toward the island's downtown section, where they took a showing of Brad Pitt and Angelina Jolie's *Mr. and Mrs. Smith* at the Nickelodeon Theater. Then they ate at Osaka Japanese Steakhouse in Harbour Town .

As Whiskey sat in the lovely oriental-themed restaurant enjoying the cutlery-tossing skills of the Tokyo-born chef, he could think of little else than killing Marcus Finbarr. Fin had cost him thousands of dollars over the past six years, and it seemed as though the Fuskie Krew had little or no answers for Fin's consistent betrayals, which angered Whiskey more than a little.

They ordered a round of rice wine, which was probably the best served anywhere in the low country. After achieving the buzz they were both looking for, they tore into their succulent dishes of teriyaki chicken and fried rice and Sapporo shrimp appetizers before the pretty Japanese waitress, clad in a gorgeous red-and-white kimono, came over smiling with the bill.

Whiskey dropped two hundred dollars for the eighty-dollar meal and helped his lovely date out of her seat, telling the waitress to keep the change.

From there, the young enforcer paid the fare for Charmaine to be taken back aboard the awaiting ferryboat toward the neighboring Daufuskie Island. He explained that he had a small business matter to attend to on the mainland. She agreed to wait up for him, and they kissed goodnight.

As the passenger yacht sailed away into the moonlit distance, Whiskey moved toward the bottom end of the wharf, where Fin's yellow-and-white yacht, *Sally Ann*, floated against the algae- and barnacle-covered docks. The light below deck was a welcome sight to Whiskey's eyes, for it let him know that his quarry was right where he knew he'd be.

He went past tipsy couples giggling and cuddling along the moon-bathed boardwalk toward *Sally Ann*, floating at the end of the pier.

Once at the bottom of the winding, wooden stairwell, the pistol-packing figure glided deftly through the shadow-dappled wharf and closed in on the yacht up ahead.

As Whiskey got within a few feet of the boat, which was bobbing up and down in the surf, he withdrew the heavy 9 mm from his waistband and quickly screwed on the silencer. The infamous Desert Eagle, noted for its fire-power and killing efficiency, was a well-known weapon of choice in the hood, drug dealers preferring it to the average 9 mm.

Whiskey slammed a fully loaded clip into the stock of the semi-automatic and carefully stepped down onto the deck of the vessel, slipping with catlike stealth through the shadows and toward the cabin below. From the light of a small lamp on a nightstand near a meager cot, he noticed Fin tapping away on a laptop as he sat on a nearby chair pulled up to a coffee table, several empty bottles of beer strewn about.

Cautiously, Whiskey tested the door handle, turning it slowly counter-clockwise. It easily opened inward towards the room.

Fin was surfing adultfriendfinder.com, chatting with a number of delectable future booty calls. He had obviously settled on a hot-looking, dark-skinned, full-figured teen cutie from Bluffton called Hotchocolate16. The twenty-eight-year-old Fin sat bare-chested and in white Fruit of the Loom briefs. He had a container of Vaseline nearby, and an unmistakable look of unbridled lust on his heavy-bearded face.

"Nigga, get yo' mufuckin' hands up in da air an' turn yo' monkey ass 'round to me!" Whiskey leveled the pistol at the shell-shocked man, who sat wide-eyed before him.

The surprised Fin quickly raised his chunky arms skyward. "You got it, you got it, my man. What you want? Money, jewelry, dis boat? Whatever it is you want, baby, you can have it, a'ight. Just lemme go." The beady little eyes of the dumpy, pot-bellied Internet porn pervert with nappy chest hair darted back and forth, searching around the room, perhaps for a weapon or some other means of self-defense or escape.

"So you been livin' large out here on Hilton Head, huh? Livin' good out here on da backs o' ya homies dat you got locked up, ain't dat right? I betcha done got ya snitch check fa da month from five-O, ain't dat right? Say somethin', you fat, greasy mufucka!"

"Who da fuck is you, dawg? Do I know you?"

"Naw, you don't know me, but I know you. You's a snitch, which makes you a bitch-ass nigga o' da worse kind, dawg. So get yo' punk ass up an' get dis boat movin' ASAP!"

Fin rose up from the chair and walked toward the door of the small cabin, his assailant trailing him with the Desert Eagle pointed at the back of his head.

"'S up? Where you wanna go, playa? Coulda least let a nigga get dressed an' shit though."

Fin tried his best to keep cool. He'd been robbed on several occasions before and had obviously come out of those uncomfortable incidents alive and well, even critically wounding one unlucky would-be stickup kid. He saw no reason why he shouldn't walk from this latest predicament unscathed.

Whiskey roughly pushed the portly yacht owner up the stairs toward the huge steering wheel overlooking the wide bow.

"You gotta untie da line on the dock befo' we can take off. I'll be ready after you undo dem ropes, a'ight?" Fin said, walking into the captain's quarters.

"Oh hell, naw!" Whiskey pulled back on the chamber of the handgun.

Clack!

"You gonna do da rope-untyin' shit, punk bitch, not me! Now get yo' fat ass on dat dock an' untie dis bitch befo' I clap dis mufucka on yo' black ass!"

"A'ight, a'ight, man! Calm down! I'm gettin' to it, okay. Just gimme a chance to go up top. But, c'mon, I'm gonna need to get my clothes befo' I go out on da dock now. C'mon! You gonna draw suspicion like dat—a buck-naked black man walkin' 'round on da wharf an' shit, gimme a break!"

Whiskey silently agreed and forced the partially nude Marcus Finbarr downstairs to fetch his crumpled clothes piled up on the floor near the cot. After Finbarr got dressed, Whiskey made him untie the slipknots tying the yacht to the dock upon the lonely bottom pier, while club hoppers frolicked with merriment several feet above them along the cobblestone paths of Hilton Head's historic nightlife venue.

"A'ight, you got yo' wish. Now where we goin'?"

"Just drive dis mufucka towards Fuskie, a'ight. An' don't stop til I tell you to, a'ight."

"Looka here, playa, like I said, if you want money, I got you. I ain't hurtin' for no paper, so just take whatever it is you want, okay? I got 'bout five grand downstairs in da hole on da nightstand in a shoebox. All you gotta do is go an' get it, but don't go an' do nothin' stupid, 'cause if anything happens to me, lemme tell ya, you gon' be in a world o' trouble."

Finbarr carefully looked over his shoulder occasionally, while pulling the yacht away from Harbour Town's wharf and out into the night waters of the moonlit Cooper River beyond.

Whiskey quickly moved up close to his hostage's left ear, pressing the muzzle of the 9 mm hard to the back of Fin's sweaty head.

"C'mon, man, all dis shit ain't called for!"

Whiskey smiled wickedly and licked his lips. Then he said softly into Fin's bat-like ear, "Just drive this boat to where I tell you and shut da fuck up. Don't say shit else, or you's one dead ass, you understand me, boy?"

Fin silently obeyed Whiskey's orders and steered his yacht toward Daufuskie's Haig Point area, leaving white caps streaking the river in his wake.

Slowly the dark silhouette of Daufuskie Island came into view. Both men were silent as the yacht's engine hummed audibly, powering the mid-sized vessel steadily towards its destination.

As the old, rugged dock came into view, Whiskey kicked Finbarr square in his wide, saggy buttocks. "I'm tired o' playin' wit' yo' dumb ass now! Get dis raggedy-ass crab trap at da dock so we can get outta here!"

Fin groaned in pain and surprise. Cussing under his

breath, he whipped the yacht into a higher gear, to add speed to the boat's approach to Daufuskie's dimly lit landing, and the engine roared, as white-capped waves broke on either side of the ship's upraised bow.

Once the boat pulled up against the weather-beaten pier, Fin quickly stepped down from the deck, closely followed by Whiskey, who pressed him forward, commanding him to fasten the vessel's ropes to the rickety wharf.

Then the two walked down the sun-bleached planks of the pier and into the humid, inky blackness of the Sea Island night.

"C'mon, snitch, walk y' ass down dis road right da fuck now!" Whiskey pushed Finbarr down the forest path.

They came upon a steep sawgrass-choked ravine bubbling over with thick quicksand sloshing about in an oatmeal-like swirl nearly twenty-seven feet deep. When Whiskey had Fin at the edge of the cliff, he leveled the muzzle of the pistol to the back of his head. "Dis is for all da soldiers who took da fall 'cause o' yo' snitchin' ass. Go to hell, where you belong, bitch!"

Fin tried to launch a desperate, empty-handed attack by lunging forward, but he was struck in the head, throat, and chest by gunshots.

Whiskey watched as Finbarr stumbled backward upon the soggy ground and clutched his chest, blood billowing out between his fat fingers. While he lay desperately, gasping for air, Whiskey walked over and stood looking down him, the man who'd single-handedly caused so much drama for him and his gangland associates for so long.

Slowly, he raised the 9 mm until its cold, hollow muzzle was level with Finbarr's head and squeezed the trigger twice, causing the heavy firearm to recoil violently with both muffled shots.

A crimson pool of gore gushed from Marcus Finbarr's shattered skull as he lay still, eyes staring upward and glazed over in a ghastly film, his mouth agape in a scream silenced by death.

Whiskey removed $227.00 from Fin's corpse before kicking the hefty body over the edge of the cliff. He smiled with wicked satisfaction as the dead informant's body plummeted to its murky grave below. He quickly stuffed the cash into his pants and placed the weapon snugly into his waistband, and then proceeded back down the muddy backwoods trail toward the dock.

Once he got back to the pier he untied the ropes and boarded the *Sally Ann* and sailed for nearly a mile and a half across the Cooper River to the marshy shores of the uninhabited Bull Island. There he dropped anchor, doused the yacht in the gasoline that had been sitting on the floor of the cabin in a large red plastic container, and torched the vessel, simultaneously boarding a small outboard rig that had been attached to the yacht for emergency purposes.

Whiskey sped away, directing the outboard motor roaring on the rear of the shallow craft, toward Haig Point. Luckily for him, he'd honed his nautical skills amongst the Gullah folk long ago during his early years as a teenage drug runner, and this boating knowledge had served him well ever since.

As the boat swiftly hurdled the river's choppy waves, a mighty explosion reverberated in the distance. He turned briefly to catch a glimpse of the bright orange fire-ball glowing brilliantly in the night sky.

Once he'd arrived ashore at Haig Point Landing, he immediately phoned Theo on his cell phone to pick him up from the dock.

Within a half-hour a pair of headlights illuminated the pitch-black darkness surrounding the winding, dirt road of Daufuskie's West End. As the vehicle drew closer the thumping, Dirty South rhymes of Young Jeezy and Lil' Wayne became clearly distinct as the shiny metallic copper-tone Porsche came to a halt in front of Whiskey.

"Damn, nigga, you been burnin' da midnight oil like a mufucka, ain't cha? Where Charmaine at?"

Whiskey opened the passenger side door and plopped down into the plush leather bucket seat. "Turn dis shit down, nigga." He lowered the volume on the radio in a quick display of irritation. "She should be home in bed by now. We went out earlier to catch a flick and get somethin' to eat afterwards. We had a pretty good time." He checked the messages on his BlackBerry.

"I know you got some o' dat ass too, didn't ya? Yeah, I know you tapped Charmaine's li'l hot ass. Dat's my cousin and I love her, but I already knew she was feelin' you from da jump. See Charmaine ain't da type o' bitch dat'll fuck a whole bunch o' niggas, but I'll tell ya what, if she like what she sees, shit, she'll throw dat young, hot pussy on yo' ass befo' you can count to three, an' dat's real talk, pimpin'."

Whiskey simply grinned, steadily scrolling through his cellular message menu. "Yeah, you called it right. I fucked her red ass," he said nonchalantly.

"I knew it. Matter o' fact, you probably hit it soon as I walked out da do' 'cause dat's just how Charmaine is. Anyway, 's up wit' you out here all by yaself at night? And how come you bringin' all o' dis mufuckin' mud an' shit up in my whip? Fuck you been doin'?—Wrestlin' gators or some shit back up in dem woods?"

Whiskey popped the glove compartment, fishing around for something to wipe off his soiled red-and-black Jordans. He found a few paper napkins and began briskly wiping off his sneakers and the surrounding carpeted floor before tossing the muddied clump of tissues out the open window.

"Let's just say I took da time to handle a situation dat shoulda been handled a long fuckin' time ago."

Theo shook his head, knowing that his friend from Georgia had just murdered someone in the backwoods they were driving away from. "Who got dealt wit'?"

Whiskey placed his BlackBerry back into its belt clip. "Punk-ass nigga name Fin. Shit, you should know 'im. He right from here on Fuskie. He used to be a top balla wit' da Fuskie Krew, 'til he started snitchin' on his peeps for da po-po a while back. He da reason why half o' dem cats on lockdown right now, including my dawgs, Joi and Nicky Stevens—Dey locked up wit' my daddy and dem at Bloody Point—not to mention how much money dat fat, nasty mufucka cost us over da years. I had ta murk his ass, ya heard."

"I feel you, baby boy. You gotta handle yours, fa sho. It ain't no other way." Theo bobbed his braided head to Juvenile's hit, "Ha," as they cruised along the darkened, dusty backroads of the sea island.

"I hope you got rid o' da body an' all o' da evidence

'cause, once da Beaufort County sheriff's office finds out he's missin', dey gon' be lookin' for his ass all over da fuckin' place."

"Don't worry 'bout a thing, dawg. Yo' boy done covered all tracks. Don't forget, I been killin' mufuckas since I been sixteen an' shit, so I ain't new to dis type o' action."

"A'ight, I'll take yo' word for it, but just remember, once you leave an' go on back to Peola, dem alphabet boys gon' come 'round here kickin' ass first an' askin' questions second. Which means us Fuskie niggas gon' have ta deal wit' five-O, not you, a'ight. Just remember dat."

"If y'all Geechee asses woulda put dat nigga's ass to sleep a while back, I wouldn't have ta come all da way from Peola to do da job, so I ain't tryin' ta hear dat bullshit. Besides, enough cops is on da dope man's payroll down here in da low-bottom Cackalack to worry 'bout da few crackas trippin' off some ol' Robocop shit, so calm yo' nerves down a spell."

"Sounds good. If I didn't know you as well as I do, I'd say you's full o' shit. But I know you's a straight soldier dat's 'bout it-'bout it, so I'm-a let it go on dat note."

"Now dat's da type o' shit I wanna hear from ya, dawg, 'cause you already know I stay trill wit' it all day, every day. Now take me to da crib so I can lay da fuck down, 'cause I'm tired dan a mufucka."

Chapter 6

"Daufuskie Day"

The Daufuskie Day celebration was in full swing that following day at the Benning's Point landing. Theo, Charmaine, Whiskey, and perhaps most, if not all, of the residents of Dunn Gardens joined the rest of the sea island's local population down at the pier, where they intermingled with the multitudes of tourists from all over South Carolina and other areas of the United States who'd come to experience the rich cultural history, savory cuisine, and lively music and entertainment of the Gullah islanders.

Old, wizened ladies bedecked in head scarves and checkered blouses made a handsome profit hawking wares such as homemade quilts, wicker baskets, and colorful straw hats, while others drew a steady flow of eager customers to their tables with the lure of island fruit wine, canned preserves, and Daufuskie's famous deviled crabs.

The island's current civic leader, county chairwoman Heather Clay shook hands with an assortment of her constituents, occasionally stopping to pose for the cluster of photographers flashing cameras in her direction.

Whiskey slowly breezed past an animated Baptist choir belting out a string of gospel standards as fan-waving spectators clapped and sang along. He scanned the entire busy riverfront area. Several local cops could be seen moving back and forth among the crowd, keeping a watchful eye out for mischievous teens or the occasional rowdy drunk. Yet, to Whiskey's disappointment, O'Malley could not be found at all. To make matters worse, even if his would-be victim had been present, the sheer number of people attending the annual event would make the police chief's murder pretty much impossible to pull off. He had no choice but to go an alternate route with his deadly plans for O'Malley, if he indeed happened to be there or showed up at some point during the festivities.

As Whiskey walked along the crowded wharf with his two colleagues, Theo caught sight of several former high-school buddies he hadn't seen in years. He excused himself to greet them and to spend time getting reacquainted.

Whiskey and Charmaine watched Theo disappear among the multitude of people as they strolled past tables topped with mouth-watering Gullah dishes.

"Sorry 'bout last night. I waited up for you as long as I could, but you must have come in early this mornin' 'cause, as you already know, I ended up fallin' asleep." Charmaine bashfully peeked over her slender shoulder at him.

"Tsk, don't even sweat dat, shawty. I didn't think you'd be up by da time I got back to da Fuskie any ol' way. I had to take care of a whole lotta shit, trust me."

"At that time of night?"

"What are you? A private detective or somethin'? Lemme just say dis, I'm a real busy man, dat's all. Bein' a college student an' all, I'm sho you can understand dat, can't ya?"

Charmaine nodded, munching on a deviled crab she'd just bought. "Hey, it's whatever. Do you, I always say." Stuffed swell, she discarded the empty shell into a nearby garbage can after finishing the last two bites of the spicy crab cake. She wiped her greasy lips and fingers briskly then turned to her companion. "Damn! Was that deviled crab good. I'm gonna get me another one. Ain't you gonna get somethin' to eat?"

Whiskey surveyed the slow-moving throng of folks walking to and fro carefully. "Naw, I ain't hungry. I'll grab a li'l somethin' later on. Right now, I'm thinkin' 'bout somethin' else altogether."

"Penny for your thoughts." She placed her hand into his as they walked along.

Considerably more cops had arrived since they came, about a dozen to be exact—Daufuskie Island Police, Hilton Head Island Police, county sheriffs and a shitload of various surrounding low country cops representing their individual departments.

Whiskey had shot probably three people while in a crowd during his entire criminal career. It was from the window of a slow-moving car during his reckless gang banging days. But that was a group of unarmed civilians he'd shot into back then. He was now much wiser. Besides, it would be a little more than foolhardy to make an attempt on the life of an armed officer while surrounded by scores of pigs.

It was evident that O'Malley would show up sooner rather than later, but even still, Whiskey's hands were tied, at least for the time being. Undeterred by the failure of his original plan, he was determined to send a lasting message to his hometown's top cop that his presence on Daufuskie was not welcome, nor would his interference with the sea islands' drug empire be tolerated any further by the underworld.

Noticing the faraway look of concern on the face of her handsome lover, Charmaine snuggled up close to Whiskey while he stopped to buy a cup of homemade lemonade.

"Umm, that looks good. Can you buy me some too? It's gettin' a little bit too hot out here now. It wasn't this hot an hour ago, don't ya think?"

Whiskey shrugged and plunked down a few extra dollars on the table of the lemonade stand.

Charmaine happily grasped the cool Styrofoam cup of lemonade from the smiling vendor. She planted a juicy kiss on Whiskey's lips before sipping a long draught of the sweet yellow concoction. "Thanks. Ya know what, Whiskey? I'm damn horny right now, and I wanna go back to my cousin's house an' fuck. I'm gonna be goin' back to school in a couple weeks, an' you're gonna probably be leavin' for Peola even sooner. So in the meantime, between time, I'm gonna get all the dick that I can possibly get 'cause, once I get back to the books, it's gonna be all about term papers and exams. Gotta take advantage of my scholarship, ya know? Anyway, I want you to fuck me as hard as you can, 'cause I like it rough. I'm a freak for pain. It's sorta my fetish, if you will. Anyway, I'm sure you won't mind beatin' my li'l coochie up, will you?"

Whiskey chuckled as Charmaine's long, painted nails grazed his broad back up and down as they stood under the shade of a wide old oak tree. "Shit, you ain't said nothin' but a word, girl"—He pulled her to his chest, his strong hands cupped across her bodaciously plump booty—" 'cause I'll fuck da shit out ya, if dat's what ya want."

"Yeah, okay, we'll see, won't we?"

"C'mon, let's get up outta here. Theo's boys will drop him off at da house. He probably ain't gonna be home no time soon anyhow."

Charmaine smiled and quickly touched the front of Whiskey's suddenly bulging cargo shorts, and the couple weaved through the dense, sweaty crowd toward the Camry parked near the island's co-op, beneath a grove of pines.

It was somewhat irritating to Charmaine that even during their raunchy lovemaking, Whiskey's mind still seemed to be on other things.

After both lovers had achieved orgasms, they both collapsed on top the satin sheets, breathing heavily for several minutes.

Charmaine smiled and eased atop Whiskey's upper body. She rested her chin on his muscular chest, running her fingers back and forth through his curly, dark chest hair, whispering sweet nothings to him, to get him to concentrate on her. But all of her feminine wiles did little to change his mind even a little bit, which only made her more frustrated.

"Look, I came down here to take care of some bidness, a'ight. I mean, you got some good pussy an' all, but dat ain't da reason I came down to Fuskie. I got mo' important shit to do."

"Nigga, fuck you!" She raised up off of his sweaty body and stood near the bed. "Go on an' do whatever it is that you and Theo usually do, which is probably drugs or some other illegal bullshit. Go on. Git, 'cause I don't wanna be a part of whatever it is that you two usually get involved in, okay. So just get your shit an' go."

Whiskey himself got up off the bed smirking. "Bitch, please . . . you ain't shit but a ho any fuckin' way, so you can't talk 'bout nobody. What you need to do is shut the fuck up wit' all dat bullshit, for real."

"Look here, li'l boy, you don't know me well enough to go callin' me outside of my name, and if anybody's a ho, it's ya mama, bitch! I think it's best for you to get your shit and go."

"This here is Theo's crib, not yours, girlfriend. It's him who invited me here, and he's da only one who can tell me to leave his house, feel me? But you ain't gotta worry 'bout me gettin' in ya way or fuckin' wit' you while I'm here 'cause, as of right now, I'm done wit' ya, shawty."

Charmaine hurled a torrent of profanities toward the brawny young thug as he gathered up his crumpled clothes from the floor and went down the hall toward the bathroom. Then she buried her head beneath the fluffy pillows and cried her eyes out.

Whiskey enjoyed a refreshing shower right before packing his bags to leave the island for home. He'd at least accomplished one of the deeds he'd set his mind to follow through with during his trip to the Palmetto state.

Though it seemed unlikely that his plan to kill the vacationing police chief would materialize, he at least wanted to return to the Daufuskie Day celebration just to set his sights on the hated O'Malley, to be assured of his physical presence on Daufuskie.

As the island taxi which he'd phoned earlier pulled up along the dusty trail in front of Theo's mobile home, Whiskey gently placed three crisp hundred-dollar bills on the cluttered coffee table and stepped out of the rickety old screen door en route to the idling taxicab without saying good-bye to his weekend lover.

Charmaine parted the venetian blinds of her room and wiped her reddened eyes as she watched the white cab pull away down the dirt road amidst a cloud of dust. "Stupid fuckin' jerk!"

As she plopped backwards onto the sex-stained sheets of the queen-sized bed, she realized that she was a fool to give herself so freely. She now officially hated men.

Whiskey stepped out of the taxi after handing him a twenty-dollar bill. The temperature had dropped to a cooler seventy-two degrees, down from the much more humid eighty-eight degrees at midday, the late-evening sun dipping like a shimmering amber disk below the coastal Carolina horizon. He'd arrived just in time to see Mickey O'Malley, pale, portly, and with a broad gap-toothed grin, as he swiped at a shock of russet hair that fell down across his high forehead and into his squinting blue eyes.

Stepping up to the makeshift podium before him, the Irishman was greeted by a hearty round of applause that lasted several minutes.

Whiskey sneered with a growing anticipation for the

chief, as he addressed the assembled onlookers in his familiar deep-voiced Bostonian accent.

O'Malley had put on considerable weight, and his rosy cheeks and red-tinged nose made him resemble a rotund leprechaun from the pages of a children's storybook.

However ridiculous the fat man seemed up on the podium cracking lame jokes in his loud yellow tropical print shirt, straw hat, and bargain basement shorts, Whiskey knew full well how formidable and unrelenting O'Malley could be when aroused to anger.

Besides bringing the people to laughter with his unique brand of humor, the chief of police received ear-splitting applause from the standing crowd, following his rousing speech declaring an all-out war on drugs and those who illicitly trafficked them on Daufuskie and throughout the surrounding low country regions, with the help of local authorities, including the Coast Guard.

As he stood along the outskirts of the boisterously cheering crowd, Whiskey realized that if something wasn't done quickly to prevent O'Malley from going forward with his objective, millions would be lost.

Whiskey checked out various spots to see if there would be any unsecured area where he could possibly pull off a quick hit-and-run shooting, but there was just no way to do that without being set upon by scores of angry boys in blue or getting shot himself. He grumbled angrily under his breath, gently toying with the trigger that lay nestled within his waistband.

While he stood staring intently at the podium up ahead, a slightly intoxicated Theo approached him, grinning and placing a beefy arm around his shoulder, sharing with him the hilarious details of his outing with his old homies. During their conversation, the matter of the kerosene came up. Theo apologized, stating that it had totally slipped his mind since he'd first requested it.

Whiskey voiced his anger at Theo for forgetting such an important matter and revealed to him the reason he needed the flammable agent in the first place.

Theo again apologized but then warned his visiting friend that the use of a Molotov cocktail to torch O'Malley's houseboat docked on the other side of the island would be a very risky move, especially since the Melrose Plantation Marina was gated and maintained by twenty-four-hour armed security.

As the waving policeman stepped down from the podium to be greeted by clapping politicians nearby, a roar of, "O'Malley for mayor! O'Malley for mayor!" went up from the crowd

Whiskey patted the bulge of the handgun's barrel in his shirt, glaring at the police chief with malice.

Then, without warning, a noisy scuffle broke out amongst the crowd between two highly inebriated young men, drawing a group of uniformed officers over to the scene of the commotion.

While the officers subdued and arrested the drunks, Whiskey moved up closer to the chief, who'd become temporarily distracted by the incident himself. Quickly sizing up the Irishman, Whiskey knew better than anyone that to try something at this point, however tempting, would be just plain old stupid. He looked over his broad shoulder at a smiling Theo, who seemed to be enjoying the unexpected drama of the alcohol-fueled fisticuffs.

Whiskey walked away with Theo back toward the taxi stand, explaining to him the not-so-happy details of his and Charmaine's breakup, which Theo shrugged off with laughter as they both entered an awaiting cab along the curb of the crowded dirt road.

Whiskey felt no disappointment at not being able to hit O'Malley this time around, knowing that within the near future the hated police chief would be dealt with.

Chapter 7

"Dirty Dixie"

David Ambrosia sat fiddling with multiple switches in front of a large mixing desk, coaxing a hard-looking young gangsta rapper's street poems directly into the microphone over the booming speaker system reverberating loudly across the two-way speakers.

"C'mon, son, you gotta speak directly into the mic, a'ight? I need to feel the shit you talkin' 'bout, so spit that shit with some conviction 'cause you a thug, right? Well, make the listeners know that. That's what you are. A'ight, give it to me. One mo' time." He took a deep drag from a bubbling water bong sitting beside him on the wide desk, clasping hands with a smiling Whiskey, who'd just entered the studio.

Whiskey had just returned to Peola that morning, and after a brief breakfast, shower, and catnap, he decided to hop in his SUV and travel on Madison Highway, taking Exit 54 toward west Peola, to get to Ambrosia's Spanish Moss Records located in Pemmican.

Usually Ambrosia would have in-house disc jockeys develop mix tapes for the various hip-hop and R&B artists signed on his label. But this particular evening the multi-platinum music producer was to be found in his studio hard at work at what he did best, next to hustling.

"A'ight, that's what the fuck I'm talkin' 'bout, son. Spit that shit with some venom. I wanna hear Pac or Biggie, not Vanilla Ice. But, anyway, that's a wrap for today. Much, much, much better," Ambrosia said, voicing his approval of the rapper's renewed verbal bravado of his album's opening track into the mic.

The aspiring rap star, no older than maybe seventeen or eighteen, placed his headphones upon the wall stand and stepped down from out of the booth. He walked over confidently toward the producer, dapping it up, hugging and laughing as they spoke about the final edits to his debut album.

As they spoke business, Whiskey helped himself to the silver-embroidered bong, coughing heavily following each toke. He placed the bong back down upon the side of the mixing board and slowly walked about the cavernous studio, checking out the numerous gold and platinum record plaques on walls about the room. He chuckled out loudly for no reason, as the Holland-grown purple haze began to take effect.

Noticing an unopened bag of nacho cheese Doritos, he quickly took hold of it and gorged on its contents with marijuana-induced gluttony.

The artist, whose stage name was No Doubt, when introduced to Whiskey, quickly asked him to rate his performance.

"I think you got skills," Whiskey told him. "You's trill

wit' yours, shawty. Just watch da hooks a li'l bit an' you'll be fine."

"A'ight, bet. So you feelin' my shit? For real though?"

Whiskey was extremely high at this point and somewhat uninterested in the teenager's rap album or career, but not wanting to diss him, he assured the grinning lyricist that he was a young Lil' Wayne in the making.

No Doubt left so pumped, he roared out the studio.

Whiskey and Ambrosia busted out laughin'.

"Remember when we in Cayman High back in the day, we used to get together with the Ballard brothers, some of them other cats from South Peola, and rock the mic on Saturdays at Da Juke Joint? So, c'mon, you already higher than a mufucka. Why don't you just step in the booth an' spit somethin' right quick?" Ambrosia said after a good laugh.

"Naw, I ain't free-styled in a while, you know. I ain't wit' all dat rap shit no mo'. I love listenin' to my Three 6 Mafia, my T.I., my Trick Daddy and shit, but I ain't 'bout ta step in nobody's booth, shawty."

"Okay, it's all good. Forget you then. Probably can't flow like you used to no how," Ambrosia said, taunting him.

"Aww, nigga, you a liar an' ya ass stink. You know I can still put it down if I wanna, but I just don't feel like it today. But I still got love for ya, though. C'mon, gimme a kiss," Whiskey said playfully.

"Yeah, your gay ass would say some shit like that, wouldn't you?" Ambrosia jokingly tapped Whiskey on the head. "Oh yeah, here take this. I almost forgot."

Whiskey stretched forth his hand to receive a personal

check from his homie totaling thirteen thousand dollars and written out to Mr. Peter Battle.

"Ya know, Whiskey, when you took out Marcus Finbarr, you did a whole lotta folks a big favor, 'specially a lot of our soldiers on lockdown. So I'm gonna bless you with this as a thank-you from all of us to you."

"You didn't have to do dat, but shit, I ain't gonna turn down no money, dat's for damn sho." Whiskey folded the check between his meaty fingers.

"You ain't supposed to." Ambrosia poured three shot glasses of Gran Patrón Platinum for himself, his homie, and all his past homies. "Ahh, Patrón, the Cadillac of tequilas."

Whiskey took the glass of the high-end tequila and pounded it back in one gulp. "I was s'pose to be takin' care o' some otha bidness, but shit didn't go da way I thought it would at all. And a whole lotta cats was bankin' on me to take care o' dat work. It's a'ight though. You know how I do it—I don't quit 'til I finish da shit."

Ambrosia slowly leaned back in his custom-made Tony Montana-themed leather chair and smiled a toothy grin, swirling the glass of Patrón around in his diamond-encrusted ringed fingers.

He looked at Whiskey. "C'mon, Whiskey, why you tryin' to keep shit all hush-hush? This is me, David, remember? We're boys, aren't we? Besides, I already know about your deal with a coupla renegade cops to Chief O'Malley. Ya know that I got contacts all across this mufucka. Son, what you think? Just 'cause I'm a white boy I can't be trusted or somethin'? Please . . . I got more hood in me than most brothas ever will have, an' you of all people know that. My late brother Lee was half black, remember, and my family grew up right outside Macon in a trailer park before moving here to West Peola. My mother was considered poor white trash by most people we knew. Even our stuck-up upper middle-class relatives disowned us because of my brother being bi-racial, and sometimes called my mom a nigga-lover to her face. It was me and my brother Lee who got out as teenagers and took our moms up outta that trailer park with hard work, both legal as well as illegal. So don't ever consider me nothing less than a brother from another mother to you, Whiskey, a'ight?"

"It's not you who I was concerned 'bout, David. It was your close bond wit' dat punk-ass O'Malley. You and dat mufucka seem to be pretty buddy-buddy an' shit last time I checked you. You even donated money to da police lodge. C'mon now, what was I s'posed ta think? It woulda been a conflict of interest tellin' you some shit like dat. Besides, it's a dirty game we're both playin' out here on dese streets. You really can't trust nobody. And trust me, no matter what you say, skin color does matter out dis bitch. Ain't shit changed since da old days. As a black man I got much mo' ta lose den you, pimp. You gotta feel me on dat one."

"True that, but I can help you, Whiskey." Ambrosia leaned forward to pour his pal yet another glass of Patrón. "I have financial interests in the coke trade goin' down on Fuskie. Who in the game right now doesn't? Dudes realize that everybody can get a piece of the pie without killin' one another, which is just plain old good business sense. And now that you know that, you realize that just because I might pose for a picture or two with

Mickey or attend an awards ceremony with the guy, it doesn't make me a fan or anything. That's just politics, a cover-up. Remember, Whiskey, always keep your enemies closer."

"Yeah, I guess ya right 'bout dat. Niggas do gotta switch dey game up every now and then."

Exhaling from the smooth heat of the tequila's trek down his throat, Ambrosia reclined into the leather seat and placed his half-empty glass down on the side of the mixing board. He touched his long pale fingers together as he settled into the leather and smiled at Whiskey from behind a pair of dark diamond-filled glasses.

"You're goddamned right, they should, 'cause it's just in everyone's best interests that we all consider doing business this way, that's all."

Taking yet another drink, he leaned forward. "So now that that's over with, how come you got Finbarr but not O'Malley? You did let certain people know that you'd have some of your homeboys handle the job, right? Well, why isn't he dead?"

" 'Cause incompetent Geechee niggas can't be depended on to do shit right, dat's why. And I couldn't get at him 'cause I happened to have come when dey was havin' dat Fuskie Day celebration. So cops was crawlin' all over da fuckin' place. A nigga couldn't just bust caps off unda dem kinda circumstances, feel me? But, don't worry, he gonna get hit sooner or later."

"I'll drink to that." Ambrosia swallowed his glass of Patrón.

"Lemme walk wit some o' dat smoke, David." Whiskey eyed the sandwich bag packed with large, smelly marijuana buds lying next to the silver bong.

"Good shit, ain't it? It's purple haze. It has a THC content of over eighty percent, real talk. I smoke nothing but the best, you know that. But yeah, sure, go ahead. Take it. It's all yours. Anyway, check it out. We gotta get down to Fuskie tomorrow 'cause I gotta meet with Snookey at the pen. He'll be glad to see you, no doubt, and for more reasons than one too." Ambrosia tossed the sealed bag of marijuana toward Whiskey, who snatched it in mid-air as he arose from his seat to leave.

"My nigga! What time tomorrow you tryin' to get down dere?" Whiskey said, looking at the crystal covering over the buds in the bag.

"Meet me here tomorrow at about noon. We'll take my private jet to Hilton Head International and then go by ferryboat from there. Got it?" Ambrosia then poured another sip of Patrón before leaving.

"A'ight, white boy, I'll holla at you 'round noon tomorrow." Whiskey smiled and tucked the smelly marijuana into his pants pocket.

Bloody Point Beach Penitentiary stood amidst the beige sand, driftwood, and deep blue surf of Daufuskie's largest beach like some old medieval castle from a monster flick. Armed guards occupied the towers above the prison yard, while others walked about stoically monitoring the daily activities of the large population of white-clad inmates. Who would think that these muscle-bound, tattoo-covered repeat offenders would give a fuck about CBS's *Pop Star* competition or *Billboard* top ten charts? Or getting rid of interfering police chiefs? No, these cats were more preoccupied with boosting their bench press or copping blowjobs from the prison's queers.

Both Whiskey and Ambrosia had done time before as juveniles, so the caged-animal atmosphere of B.P.B. prison was not unfamiliar to them.

As a long black limo pulled up to the tall wrought iron gates, the two young men emerged from the idling vehicle and entered the slowly opening gates. They were immediately searched and escorted into the facility by two heavyset guards. The guards followed closely with M-16's tightly gripped in their hands, ready for anything.

Once inside the lobby, Ambrosia nudged Whiskey and pointed to a small group of inmates sitting around a circular table near the far end of the room playing poker under a dangling ceiling lamp that illuminated every one of the card players' faces in the dim lobby.

As they approached the card table, everyone warmly embraced each other.

"My nigga. Hey, y'all, dis right here is my son, Whiskey, and my little homie, David, baddest mufuckin' cracka on dese streets right now." Snookey raised up and draped his powerful arms around Ambrosia and Whiskey.

The tall, muscular Marion "Snookey" Lake had packed on more than twenty-five pounds of muscle since he'd been imprisoned in 1994. Already a large man, he now looked absolutely colossal. Snookey was one of the most infamous street legends to come out of the Deep South, and was widely known for his ill-gotten wealth, voracious womanizing, and hair-trigger temper. It was rumored that the former New Orleans drug lord had murdered well over 175 people from 1983 to 1994, and according to his autobiography, *Hate the Game, Not the Playa*, sixty-six by his own hand.

"Boy, c'mon here. Give ya pops a hug. I ain't seen yo' li'l ass in 'round 'bout, what, a year or mo'?"

"Naw, man, I seen you six months ago, Snookey. You done forgot already. C'mon, ya ain't dat damn old now."

"Six months? Dat's all? Well, when niggas on lock like us, we kinda forget shit somewhat, ya feel me?"

"So, Snookey, me and Whiskey tryin' to get down to some business, if you don't mind, 'cause we think you want to hear what we got goin' on." Ambrosia pulled up a chair near the wall and sat himself at the table amongst the hard-looking jailbirds, who eagerly awaited the white boy's speech.

A short, round fellow with horn-rimmed glasses and a neatly trimmed beard tapped his manicured nails incessantly against the top of the plastic folding table. He stood up and shook hands with both Whiskey and Ambrosia. "Gentlemen, I've heard many good things about you both. I'm Patrick Dutton. I do all of the computer troubleshooting around this joint. I'm sort of the prison techno geek, if you will."

Then a tall, distinguished-looking man of about fifty-four with a strong, square jawline, wavy salt-and-pepper hair, and smooth, dark skin reached across the table over the cards to touch fists with the pair. " 'S up? My name's Lawrence Tate, but these cats on the inside just call me Tate."

Whiskey knew from Ambrosia that Larry Tate was once a lieutenant on the LAPD who had gotten busted back in the eighties along with several other crooked cops who'd been found guilty of drug trafficking, money laundering, coercion and murder, in cahoots with Colombian cartel boss, Sergio "Big Daddy" Mendez and his violent militia men. He now partnered up with the Lake

Clan, running drugs throughout Bloody Point's west wing.

Next to the disgraced LA cop sat the leader of Daufuskie's Fuskie Krew, Joi Stevens, who pushed his chair back and embraced both men, especially Whiskey, with love. Tall, rangy, and nearly blue-black in complexion, he'd known both Whiskey and Ambrosia for many years, dealing narcotics and illegal firearms.

"Sup witcha, Joi?" Whiskey asked after embracing his imprisoned homie.

"Ain't shit. Just tryin' ta make dis money an' to get da fuck up outta da pen is all." Joi turned to Ambrosia and placed a stack of rubber band-wrapped bills in his hands.

Snookey pointed. "This is my man Nicky. He's Joi's brother, as you probably already know, and this li'l skinny white boy right here is Peckawood. He is our own personal li'l snitch up here in da west wing, ya heard me?"

"I know all dese jailbirds, Snookey. I'm just ready ta get down ta some bidness here today, dang!" Whiskey responded. "So can we cut all da reunion bullshit an' get started?"

Snookey Lake 's face soured into a frown at the blunt words of his estranged son before he again resumed a calm, smiling demeanor.

"Yeah, Snookey, I agree wit' da kid. C'mon an' let's do dis," Joi said, " 'cause I can't wait to hear what dey talkin' 'bout."

Whiskey grabbed his chair and plopped down into it next to Ambrosia and Joi. Next to his old man Snookey, Peckawood and Nicky seated themselves simultaneously into the now crowded card table.

Correction officers stood guard over the impromptu business meeting, making sure that no one interfered or questioned the purpose of the gathering.

Snookey and the rest of the Lake Clan had the entire west wing on lock, buying protection and silence from the guards concerning their illicit in-house operations, and gaining special favors.

"Hey, look, we want y'all li'l mufuckas to know dat da C.O.'s ain't gonna bite cha, 'cause we break dese bitches off too damn good fo' dat hot shit. Ain't dat right, Marcus?"

The tall, wiry prison guard chuckled along with the wisecracking Snookey Lake and flipped him the middle finger all at the same time.

"Yeah, a'ight. It's like dat? Dat's why I'm gonna tell everybody dat you been suckin' on dis wood befo' you clock out every day, ya faggy-ass *beeaatch*!"

Everybody at the table busted out into raucous laughter at the kingpin's witty putdown of the broadly smiling guard, who continued to be peppered by the biting remarks of the suddenly jovial Snookey, who seemed to relish in the heavy laughter as well as the C.O.'s inability to counter his verbal assaults.

Then, just as suddenly as he'd begun the impromptu comedy session, he stopped dead silent, while the chuckling slowly died around him.

Staring directly at his seed and Ambrosia, Snookey spoke slowly, "Y'all makin' a li'l bit o' money back home, I heard. Been hearin' a whole lotta good shit 'bout y'all boys, 'specially Davey right here. Done gone an' got hisself a record label an' shit. I see some been learnin' a thing or two by watchin' da Snookey's hustle, huh. I'm proud o' ya, white boy. Now talk to me. What y'all got on ya mind?"

Ambrosia quickly dropped a tall stack of money upon the hard plastic tabletop and leaned his elbows forward on the table. "That right there is about, what, five grand? Yeah, five grand. That's my gift to da Lake Clan, especially you, Snookey, 'cause I wanna show you some love 'cause this one hustle is more important than any one deal you've ever closed."

Snookey leaned back into his chair, which was engulfed by his mammoth frame. He lit up a Salem cigarette and took a long drag on the menthol cancer stick. "Looka here, I know all about yo' hustle, da record sales, da singas and rappas, I know all o' dat shit." He exhaled a heavy cloud of smoke and stared at the youngsters through bloodshot eyes. "I know that you two didn't come down here to see us just fa GP, so lay it on us."

"Well, I'll just start of with thankin' y'all for gettin' with us today." Ambrosia smiled. "We've got a problem here on Daufuskie, as y'all already know. Whiskey came down here a li'l while ago to take care of O'Malley, but since it was during the time of the Daufuskie Day celebration, he couldn't peel his cap like he would've usually. But, of course, we're still gonna make sure that we get the job done 'cause O'Malley's costing all of us a lot of money, not just the Lake Clan."

The other inmates nodded in agreement with the white boy.

"So you all know that we gonna do da damn thing, but as they say, shit happens."

"Y'all betta, 'cuz we got over a million dollars worth o' coke s'posed ta be comin' in round 'bout December, so we don't need no mo' fuckups when it comes to gettin' rid o' this cop, period!" Joi said in a matter-of-fact manner.

"Ya know what, Joi? I feel your concern wit' da job bein' done correctly, I really do. But you know how I do shit. An' if you know dat, you know damn well dat don't nobody I set my sights on ta hit ever, ever get away. So you just remember dat befo' you come out at me wrong next time, playa," Whiskey said loud and clear.

Whiskey's sire flashed a broad grin that showed his diamond- and gold-encrusted teeth, in acknowledgment of his son's courage. "Dat's what da fuck I'm talkin' 'bout. Don't take shit off nobody, Whiskey, 'cause you's my son, an' I don't make no punks. But, for real though, it ain't hard to get O'Malley hit. I done got plenty o' cops touched back in da day when I was livin' in New Orleans. All I had to do was give a pipehead a coupla rocks, an' he or she would put dat pig ta sleep. So if y'all want help, in dat case it ain't nothin' but a phone call away."

Whiskey stared at his father unflinchingly. "I already got a coupla li'l hardheads ready ta put in work already, so I don't need nobody's fuckin' help."

"Yeah, okay. I'm tryin' ta help you out, li'l mufucka, 'cause you don't want just anybody doin' da job on a police chief. 'Cause, you betta believe, if you don't have a mufucka to take dat heat fo' you, you ain't never gonna see da light o' day again."

"Okay, now that is over with, obviously you cats got something or someone up your sleeve. Let's hear it," said an anxious David Ambrosia.

Whiskey shook his head. "Oh naw, David, ever since my methods been questioned an' shit, I wanna know how da Lake Clan can do a betta job at gettin' rid o' O'Malley. Dat's what I wanna know."

Joi lit up a cigarette. "Okay, bet. All we gotta do, for real, is to pay off one o' dese crooked cops on da island who work for the Daufuskie police department. I know a few o' dem dudes myself, an' dey got money tied up in dis cocaine bidness we runnin' from down in Miami. So work ain't gonna be hard."

"Yeah, I'm feelin' dat move mo' dan any other one," Snookey said. "Dat's what's up."

"Great. Let's get this cop on the payroll quick, 'cause we need this hit to happen now," Ambrosia said.

Peckawood said from the far end of the card table, near the wall, "Getting O'Malley hit ain't a problem, but murder-for-hire costs money, a lotta money. Now whoever we choose from the force to kill this sonofabitch is surely gonna cost us an arm an' a leg. Now I know for a fact the Lake Clan's gonna hold up their end of the cost, but how can we be certain that you guys are gonna be able to afford your part?"

David asked, "Y'all got enough paper to cover yo' end?"

"Look, y'all can pay some cop a shitload o' money to off dis cat, who just might snitch when it's all said an' done regardless, or y'all can pay me an' David sixty grand even, which we'll split 'tween us down da middle, an' I guarantee you da job will get done, 'cause dese dudes dat I use ain't nothin' but gutter-ass ex-cons who'd love nothin' more than to push a cop's wig back fa free. So you know what they'll do fa a coupla hundred dollars."

Ambrosia touched clenched fists with his friend in

agreement. "I know you all feel Whiskey on this one. We all know that he's about his work, at least most of us at this table. Trust me, if this man says he's gonna do something, believe me, he's gonna."

Peckawood conversed softly with Lawrence Tuppince, as Ambrosia finished up his dialogue.

"Sixty gees is a whole lot just to kill some stupid cop, don't cha think?" Peckawood scoffed.

"Oh yeah? Well, how much do you think dat police officer y'all thinkin' 'bout usin' woulda charged ya? I guarantee ya he'd go higher than sixty gran' to take his boss out. He'd probably hit y'all's pocket with anywhere from eighty-five to a hundred gran' easy, considerin' da stakes involved. I gotta take risks here my damn self, no matter who pulls da trigger. So da price stands at sixty thousand dollars, and dat's it and dat's all." Whiskey crossed his arms in front of him.

Joi snickered. "For sixty gran'? Shit, y'all betta bring back dat mufucka's dick and balls fa proof, dawg. You my man, Whiskey. You know you are, but hey, dis is bidness, and we gotta hire da best man fa da job 'cause niggas ain't payin' nobody dat kinda loot fa mistakes."

"Amen to dat, my brotha!" Snookey winked at Whiskey across the table. "I think fifteen thousand is more than enough. For sixty thousand dollars you'd betta kill da whole goddamned police force."

"Ya see, y'all mufuckas up here bullshittin', but as soon as Chief O'Malley gets the fundin' to beef up Fuskie's police department, y'all gonna be sittin' round' lookin' stupid 'cause he gonna put all o' dis big-ballin' shit y'all got goin' on down here to rest. Trust me, I know how dat

Irish mufucka rolls," Whiskey said, his irritation growing. " 'Specially you, Snookey, you know how hard O'-
Malley go. I know da connections y'all got down in
Miami, Dade County, as well as y'all's Richmond, VA
connects. Dem dudes ain't gonna keep fuckin' wit y'all if
y'all let O'Malley make da block hot down here in Souf
Cack. I damn well ain't tryin' ta blow over a million dollars worth o' Colombian flake comin' from Florida, nor a
hundred gran' in heroin and crystal meth comin' down
from Richmond an' Tidewater, VA. Dat's too much
money to fuck up. Besides, da MS-13 already gettin' dey
game plan together to cash in on dat money from Char-
lotte an' Orlando just as soon as O'Malley's drug task
force shut down all dope operations down in da low
country. So y'all can sit here politickin' over nickels an'
dimes if ya want . . . 'cause, for real, in da long run all o'
y'all country-ass niggas gon' lose out fuckin' wit' punk-
ass Mickey O'Malley."

"Now that he's laid it to us like that, the kid just might
have a point there." Peckawood ran his pale, thin fingers
through his unkempt sandy brown hair.

Whiskey whispered with Ambrosia, while the inmates
powwowed with each other at the table, trying to come
to a final decision on the matter at hand.

"Look, y'all, I came here 'cause David asked me to
come. Either y'all dudes down, or you ain't, it's dat simple. 'Cause I dunno 'bout David, but I got better things to
do than to hang around a jailhouse all day long."

Snookey took one final drag off the cigarette before
smashing it down into an ashtray beside him. He cleared
his throat to speak, his gaze fixed upon both Ambrosia

and his son. "A'ight, since you so sho dat you can murk O'Malley's fat ass, we gonna foot da bill dat you askin' 'cause I got too much money tied up wit' my Florida and Virginia connects to let dis cracka fuck it up. You absolutely right 'bout dat shit. But dis ain't a job fa no standin'-on-da-corner, wannabe gangsta punks or no half-baked, braindead dope addict neither. Dis shit gotta be done right, and it gotta be done quick . . . 'cause you my son and I fucks wit' you. But I ain't toleratin' no fuck-ups from you or nobody else, you understand? You either get da job done or don't even go there, 'cause we ain't givin' you sixty thousand dollars for nothin'.'"

"Look, guys, Whiskey is not only my friend, but he's a pro when it comes to killin' cats. He's disposed of quite a few rats, rivals, and overdue customers for me during the past several years, so I know what this guy is capable of. Trust me, your money will be well spent." Ambrosia looked over toward Whiskey, who sat back in his seat with his beefy arms folded across his chest and winked, all the while smiling confidently.

Lawrence Tuppince shrugged his shoulders and nodded his head in agreement with the other convicts at the table.

"A'ight then, you got yaself a deal, boy." Snookey shuffled the deck of playing cards in his hand.

The lanky corrections officer stood silent, except for a slight smile creasing the corners of his broad mouth when Peckawood eased a hundred-dollar bill into his back pocket as he kept watch over the illicit dealings.

"Hey, David, 's up wit' cha girl, Godiva? Word on da street is, since she been blowin' up on dat TV show, *Pop Star*, you been takin' notice. *Entertainment Tonight* last week aired a segment about da *Pop Star* finale, sayin' you was gonna sign her on to a contract after da competition. If so, I wanna piece o' dat action, 'cause da bitch can sing her ass off and she got star quality. I need to invest some o' dis dirty money in some good ol' clean bidness. Why not da music bidness?" Snookey asked.

Ambrosia laughed briefly. "Yeah, she's the hottest thing next to Beyoncé right now, and she hasn't even won the final competition on *Pop Star* yet. I was surprised that no other producer had signed the chick. But, hey, their loss is definitely my gain. And to answer your question, I totally would want to be partners with you in this music venture."

"Godiva? Music? C'mon, Snookey, quit playin', dawg. We got shit locked down with our dope hustle. Why da fuck we need ta put our money into R&B shit? Who da fuck you think you is? Berry Gordy?" Joi shook a cigarette into his palm from a newly opened pack.

"See, dat's da shit I'm talkin' 'bout. Y'all ghetto-ass mufuckas don't know shit 'bout no real bidness. All y'all know 'bout is how ta sling rocks an' then buy up a shit-load o' whips, spinnin' rims, and gold chains an' shit. Ya know what the Italians I used to fuck wit' call dat? *Nigga rich*—Yeah, dat's what dem mafia boys used to say. Whenever dey saw one o' us step outta pimped-out truck with gold 'round dey necks and stylish clothes on, dem Italian crackas would bust out laughin'. Ya wanna know why?" Snookey asked. " 'Cause everybody know niggas love ta buy shit, but they don't invest in shit. 'Cept niggas who know da rules o' da game like me. Ya see, money launderin' is da backbone o' da game. If you ain't got a legit hustle ta hide ya dirty money behind as a smokescreen, you's one dumb mufucka. An' it can't be no obvious shit either. Laundromats, liquor stores, and car dealerships, da feds jump on dem joints like stink on shit, 'cause everybody done bought one o' dem in da hood. Even fast-food joints is hot nowadays, but if you put up money in some big-time classy shit like a five-star restaurant, or a fancy hotel on a resort island, or in dis case a nationally known record label dat's 'bout ta sign da next singin' sensation ta come along since Aaliyah, and she's a white girl too. Who in dey right mind gonna think dat a bunch o' dope-hustlin' cons down in a Souf Cackalack pen is funnelin' drugs behind the scenes?"

Peckawood glanced at the still unsure Gullah prisoner, while leaning over to speak. "Joi, ya gotta consider this, man. We'd always have money comin' in, even if our drug spots get busted or we lose connects on the outside. David's got a nationally recognized record label that makes stars outta average singers and rappers, and now he's about to sign Godiva O'Sullivan. Shit, man, that gal's gonna take the fuckin' industry by storm, you just watch. Hell, she's on every television show and commercial now, not to mention hearin' just about every last one of her songs on the radio. And this kid hasn't even won the *Pop Star* competition yet. C'mon, Joi, we can't look a gift horse in the mouth, for Christ sakes!"

"Whatever."

"Anyway, I know my pops is familiar wit' da Forrester girls from Hilton Head. Them two bitches will murk dey own mama if da price is right, and dey top-flight when it comes to puttin' heads to bed. So get at me wit' da cash no later than August eleventh, an' we'll do da damn thang. It's July twenty-eighth right now, so time's a-wastin'."

"Sounds like a plan to me." Snookey raised up from his chair to embrace the two young men, and his fellow inmates followed suit.

Snookey walked his two visitors over toward the guards waiting at the exit door of the visitors' center. "So what y'all li'l hardheads 'bout ta get into once y'all leave here?"

"Shit, I dunno what David gonna do, but I'm gonna go clubbin' out at da Sand Dollar Lounge tonight. I heard T-Pain, Akon, and Young Jeezy gonna bring mo' bitches than a little bit out dat joint. I needs ta get my dick wet, so somebody's daughter gon' git stuck tonight."

"Well, as for me, I gotta meet with a few music executives in Manhattan tomorrow morning around nine. Then I gotta get back to Peola to take care of some paperwork and fly out around midnight or so. Unlike some people, some of us gotta really work for a living." Ambrosia jokingly nudged his friend.

Snookey strolled out toward the awaiting limousine with the two young men before stopping at the gate's entrance. "A'ight, handle ya bidness, ya heard me? Act like you know," he said, as the great iron gates slowly closed behind the departing visitors.

Chapter 8

"Big Dough"

A wind of change on August 29, 2005, a monstrous Category 5 hurricane dubbed Katrina, slammed into New Orleans with the force of a hellish sledgehammer, flooding up to eighty percent of the Crescent City with a devastating deluge and transforming it into a modern-day Atlantis that took away the lives of over a thousand residents, not to mention breaching several levees and causing $81.2 billion in damages, making it one of the greatest natural disasters in modern US history. Hurricane Katrina, which ranked as the sixth strongest hurricane on record, had the local residents scrambling for higher ground, including entire families stranded on rooftops, trees, and cars for a week or more.

The New Orleans Superdome became a haven for both the vulnerable as well as the predatory during the extended neglect from President Bush and FEMA, while looting and violent crime became so widespread that the National Guard and law enforcement officers from Louisiana as well as the rest of the US were brought into the city to restore law and order as the Red Cross went about their rescue and recovery business.

Mickey O'Malley immediately shifted his attention from the drug trafficking woes of Beaufort County's low country to the hurricane and crime-ravaged streets of New Orleans. On September 14, Chief O'Malley along with thirty of Peola, Georgia's finest officers arrived in the city for an extensive tour of duty. In his absence, lead detective, Courtney O'Malley, thirty-five-year-old daughter of the police chief, was appointed, to the dismay and irritation of many a veteran Peola beat cop. They'd considered their chief's act of nepotism unfair to the elder high-ranking officers who'd served on the department much longer than the attractive Harvard-educated youngster.

Singleton Beach was one of Whiskey's favorite hangout spots whenever he was visiting the Sea Islands. There the music tended to be upbeat, the food scrumptious, and the women willing and wanton. He enjoyed the festive atmosphere of the beach at night, particularly when the management hosted a special event such as the popular Beach Fest concert, which drew hundreds of low country youths of all ethnicities. As usual he'd paid for VIP tickets for the two-and-a-half-hour celebration.

As he enjoyed the final performance of the night by UGK from the back of the bar, a hulky Filipino-looking bodyguard approached and informed him that Godiva, who'd performed earlier to a standing ovation, wanted to have a drink or two with him backstage in her dressing room. After downing a tall glass of Rémy Martin on

the rocks, he raised up off of the barstool on which he sat
and followed the bodyguard through the dense crowd of
young adults dancing barefoot upon the sandy beach,
several huge bonfires burning brightly in the background
all around them. He was ushered into a long blue-and-
white RV, where the lovely, long-haired blonde sat cross-
legged upon a leather couch, swirling a glass of
champagne in her hand.

"Peter Battle, right? It's a pleasure to finally meet you.
David talks about you all the time, so I decided to sorta
introduce myself to you personally tonight after he told
me you'd be here. So, would you like a drink? 'Cause
there's plenty here." She giggled lightly before sipping
her champagne.

"Yeah, that's what's up. I'll take a glass o' Moet, and
please call me Whiskey, okay?" He pulled up a seat against
the wall, beside the table that was laden with liquor bottles.

"Oh, my bad. Whiskey, you know what . . . have we
met somewhere before? You look really familiar."

"Yeah, you used to strip at da Strokers Club up in ATL.
A couple o' years ago you was da only white girl who
stripped for 'em. Shit, I remember you used ta be one o'
da top girls in da Strokers Club. Ya used ta be my favorite, dat's fa damn sho. I used ta drop a couple o' hunit
on you alone. I ain't never had a lap dance like da ones
you'd give a nigga."

She smiled broadly. "That's where I remember you
from. You were the big baller who was always tryin' to
get into my pants," she said, her voice slurring a bit from
intoxication. "But, hey, you definitely weren't the only
guy tryin' to fuck me, though. I'd say, I got hit on after

every show. In fact, all the girls got propositioned by the customers. It just goes with the territory, I guess. Some of the girls would take a customer up on a sex-for-hire offer if the price was right. I even know a girl who had one particular customer pay her rent and her way through college. I never did have sex with customers, though, no matter how much money or how hot a guy looked. Stripping for me was strictly business. Besides, I heard more than a few horror stories about dates gone bad with customers."

"I feel you. But I coulda got you even wit'out givin' up no paper, 'cause I know you was feelin' a nigga fa sho. I almost had you twice, but you always backed out at da last minute, talkin' 'bout how you was already in a relationship, or some other bullshit story. You know you wanted me." Whiskey took a drink from the glass of bubbly he'd just poured for himself. "You lucky you my man's girl or else you'd be in real trouble wit' a pussy-hound like me."

"Is that so? Well, guess what . . . David and I are engaged, yes, but married, no. Besides, I don't think you could handle li'l ol' me anyway, *Whiskey*."

"I'm gonna take that as the alcohol talkin'." Whiskey admired the songbird's shapely legs, which she seductively crossed and uncrossed periodically during their conversation. " 'Cause I know, and you do too, dat you talkin' crazy, don't you?"

During their discussion she noticed Whiskey checking out her bare legs and decided to give him a brief glimpse of her bushy blonde pubic hair, reminiscent of a Sharon Stone scene in the movie *Basic Instinct*.

Whiskey finished up the last swallow of champagne

before filling his wine glass with more of the pricey booze and moving across the room beside Godiva.

"I was wondering how long it would take you to sit down next to me. I guess the fact that I'm not wearing any panties does the trick, huh?" She stared at him with a beckoning glint to her baby blue eyes. "You used to try really, really hard to get me in bed with you back in my Strokers Club days. Who knows, tonight you just might get your wish."

"A part of me wanna go dere wit' cha, but then again, wit' you bein' engaged to David, I dunno if I kin do dat. But I gotta tell ya, I'm a man first, and you makin' it real hard for me to get up and go outta dat do' wit'out puttin' dis dick up in you. I ain't lyin'."

"David? Gimme a break. Even though we're engaged, our relationship is more of a business arrangement than anything else. He met me two years ago when I was dancing nude at the Strokers Club, just as you and hundreds of other men over the years. Except, during the time we got to know each other, he discovered my talent as a singer, and with the *Pop Star* competition promising me a record deal after the grand finale, he is a great manager, a wonderful friend. Sure, I love David with all of my heart, but our sex life totally sucks. He's always on the go. New York on Monday, LA on Tuesday, and God knows where during the rest of the week. Tell me, do you think for one single minute that a young, hot-looking guy like David is not sleeping around on me during those many weeks away from me? Yeah, right! He's probably got a slut or two in every city just waiting for him whenever he arrives. I wasn't born yesterday, ya know. We might have sex twice a month, if am lucky. Besides, I like black guys in the sack anyway. My daughter's daddy is black, and nothing fills me up like a long, thick, beautiful, black cock. And you know what? I really think he knows that, deep down inside. He knows I have sexual needs that he's not meeting, so I feel that he'd rather have his best friend fuck me rather than me sleep with a stranger or groupie."

Whiskey licked his full lips, his wood stiffening within his boxers. "So what's up? You ain't gotta talk no mo'. I'm convinced, or sold, or whatever da fuck you wanna call it. I'm tryin' to scratch dat itch ya got, feel me?" He brushed away her golden locks from her soft neck, nibbling along its length, and kneading her large breasts delicately in his thick hands.

"Oh yeah. Don't stop. I want to feel you inside me."

Whiskey quickly removed his lengthy, heavily veined, uncircumcised member from within his jean shorts and drove it deep within Godiva's hot pink snatch, causing the blonde bombshell to gasp with pleasure as she wrapped her curly legs around his waist.

"Take dis big black dick. Ride it like you want it. Ride da dick, baby, ride it!"

"Oh my god, you're so fuckin' big. You're a stud, baby. Oh good god, yeah. Don't stop! It feels sooo good!"

"Oh fuck! Dat's what I'm talkin' 'bout. Fuck me back, baby. Put ya back into it!" He grunted, thrusting with primal gusto, causing Godiva to squeal out in sexual bliss as her body quivered through multiple orgasms.

Whiskey withdrew his penis from Godiva's sticky, wet pussy to shoot a heavy load of creamy, white goblets onto her abdomen and boobs.

Afterwards the two lovers cuddled together, sweaty

and naked on the cum-stained couch, sipping on champagne, and listening to the festivities on the beach beyond.

Robbie Stevens, the younger brother of the incarcerated Joi, and Nicky resided on Wild Horse Road, in an old, weather-beaten mobile home that stood alone against a dense forest of tall pine trees and the rusty ruins of junked cars. The neighborhood was Spanish Wells, a predominantly black section of Hilton Head, known as "Da Wells" by drug-dealing thugs and addicts. Several snot-nosed brats romped about among the broken-down rust buckets as a scrawny, mixed-breed coon dog ran behind them, barking and playfully nipping at their heels as they zigzagged back and forth.

Whiskey exited his Jeep Cherokee and walked up the rickety steps and through the flimsy screen door to loudly announce his presence. Nicky emerged from the back, bare-chested and with blunt in hand to greet Whiskey.

"My nigga, 's up wit' cha, boy?"

"Ain't shit. I see you all back up in da cut and shit wit' cha li'l daycare."

"Aw, nigga, fuck you. You know fa sho all dem mufuckin' chillen ain't hardly mine. Just dese two right here, an' dat's all."

"A'ight, damn. Shit, I dunno, y'all Geechee niggas, like President Bush, don't believe in pullin' da fuck out."

"Keep talkin' shit and I'm-a tell ya mama she gon' have ta work a extra two hours on da ho stroll tonight."

Whiskey chuckled at Nicky's quick comeback and

vowed to launch a counterattack when he least expected it.

Stepping through the threshold of the trailer, Nicky turned toward Whiskey and offered him the blunt as they entered.

"I know ya stankin' ass wanna hit dis mufucka, don't cha? Well, puff on it wit' caution, shawty, 'cause dis dat Sea Island funk, baby. Only thoroughbred niggas kin take dis shit."

Whiskey flashed his Gullah homie a quick smirk and snatched the blunt from his calloused outstretched hand.

Inside, cheap wicker-wood furniture stood out within the drab, musty interior of the mobile home. Broken toys littered the living room floor, along with several doggie chew bones and a big bag of bacon-flavored Alpo. The kitchen was untidy, smelled of stale malt liquor, and was dark, with the exception of the glowing red numbers displayed on the microwave.

"Damn, nigga! Don't you ever clean up dis raggedy mufucka?"

"I don't live here. Dis my baby-mama crib and shit. She da triflin' one, not me. I'm just over here to make sure everything is straight, while she make a run out to Savannah to pick up her sister." Nicky took a puff on the blunt again.

"Dat's some good shit, Nicky. Y'all da only dudes I know who got da bomb-ass homegrown bud. You gon' gimme a couple ounces o' dis Geechee weed to sell back home in Peola, a'ight? How much ya want for three ounces o' dis shit?"

"For you, lemme see . . . I'll let cha have five ounces for

seven fifty. You a'ight wit' dat?" Nicky handed Whiskey the smoking roach. "Follow me to the bedroom. It's in da closet back here. Then I want you to meet my man Bubby. He lives over yonder cross da road a ways. He represent da Fuskie Krew, just like me. He also pushin' weight. Matter o' fact, he move mo' bricks 'round here den anybody."

Whiskey followed Nicky through the untidy living room, down the narrow hall, and into the cramped and humid back room. Not wanting to go any further, he stood at the doorway, while Nicky trudged through a smelly assortment of dirty laundry before opening the closet door and lifting a hefty sandwich bag filled with marijuana from between pairs of sneakers and patent leather pumps from the top shelf.

Like a gray flash, a cat suddenly raced from beneath the bed and through Whiskey's legs, momentarily startling the two men.

After Whiskey purchased the cannabis, the two young men hopped in Whiskey's Jeep and drove seven houses up the dirt road and pulled up into the cobblestone driveway of an impressive triple-wide mobile home that seemed more mini-mansion than high-end trailer.

The two friends were greeted at the door by Bubby, a handsome, narrow-faced gentleman in his fifties. He welcomed the guests into the spacious living room, which bore a sweet aroma of pink grapefruit potpourri, Floetry playing softly in the background.

Two highly attractive women sat upon the beautiful crushed velvet couch smiling broadly, periodically stepping to sniff the thin, neatly placed lines of white powder on a glass plate before them.

"You must be Whiskey. How you doin'? C'mon and have a seat. Y'all want some blow?" Bubby asked as his young guests sat down on the luxurious couch beside the smiling beauties.

Nicky took his host up on his offer and wasted little time joining the giggling girls in snorting up several lines of coke.

Whiskey said, "I'm good. Thanks anyway. My man Nicky tells me dat you rep Fuskie. You gotta be an OG. How long you been runnin' wit da Krew?"

"Shit, I'd say, I've been down wit' da Krew since seventy or seventy-one."

"Dat's wassup." Whiskey pounded fists with the older gangsta. "I been fuckin' wit' da Krew for a minute now, and dem boys like my family, know what I'm sayin'? Like family."

Bubby smiled slightly. "Nicky told me dat y'all go way back. Dat's good to know, 'cause anybody who's a friend of Nicky is a friend o' mine, and I don't have many. But da ones I do have, believe me, dey benefit from the association . . . greatly." Bubby bent down to snort a line with a tightly rolled hundred-dollar bill. "You down here for a while or what?"

"Naw, I'll be outta here by tonight or early tomorrow morning. I just came down to visit my pops, dat's all."

"Dat's what a son is s'ppose to do, ain't dat right, girls?"

The women both responded with a simultaneous, "Yes," smiling all the while with toothy grins.

"Ya see my girls Latrice and Mercedes over there? Dey some kinda fine, ain't dey? Dey been takin' care o' big daddy since two thousand, an' if you look 'roun' here at dis place I got, I'd say dese pretty gals is doin' a fairly good job at it, don't ya think?"

"Fa sho." Whiskey glanced over at the girls.

Mercedes winked an eye at him. "C'mon, sit down an' party wit' us, y'all. We can't possibly toot all o' dis powda by ourselves, now can we?"

"I gotta tell ya, I don't do coke. My mama was a coke addict, ya see. Flake, rocks, it didn't matter to her none, long as she got high. She'd rather chase dat white horse dan feed her own chillen. If it wasn't for my sister LaTasha, we'd probably starve to death. I might drink like a fish and smoke hella weed, but I don't do no hard dope 'cause I seen what kinda damage it done to my mama. So now I just sell da shit, an' dat's it."

After a brief, awkward silence Mercedes, the more outspoken of the two girls, cleared her throat while dividing a small heap of cocaine with a playing card. "I'm so sorry, baby. We didn't know. I hope we didn't offend you. I apologize for everybody, boo, believe dat."

Whiskey slowly shuffled the deck of cards, focusing on her bulging cleavage as much as her apologetic words. "You ain't gotta apologize for nothin', sweetheart. Once we all get grown, we got da free will to do whatever. So please don't feel sorry 'bout da situation, 'cause she did it to herself."

Latrice sniffed a pinch of coke from a tiny spoon. "You ain't lyin'. We all reap what we sow, dat's for damn sure."

Nicky brought up the question of money. "Looka here, Bubby, remember dat crystal meth deal back in April when I drove a shitload o' dat product to Raleigh, North Carolina to close it with dem white boys up dere? Ya know, you only paid me eight hunit. When is you gonna pay me da rest o' da twelve hunit you owe me?"

"C'mon, Nicky, we've been through dis song an' dance befo', young man. I explained to you dat eight hundred would be da final and only payment fo' dat particular deal 'cause dat client only paid for that single delivery. Plus, you know as well as I do dat we don't do bidness wit' dem folks no mo', right. So don't ask me 'bout dat shit no mo', Nicky, okay?"

Whiskey noticed how uncomfortable Nicky looked behind Bubby's response, yet the Gullah youth did little afterwards, except sit between the girls and look dejected and saddened.

Latrice placed a bejeweled hand upon Nicky's cheek and stroked his stubbly jaw slowly. "It's okay, baby, you know Bubby will make sure he takes care o' you. Don't he always?"

"Yeah, suga. Besides, you run all da coke bidness from Hilton Head all da way to Charleston for Big Daddy, don't cha? And whenever he make a big score, you know da first person he gonna call on ta go get dat paper."

Whiskey sprinkled a twenty-dollar bag of cannabis into the empty husk of a Dutch Masters cigar he'd just opened and folded it into a perfectly rolled blunt before licking the loose ends shut.

"I heard that you pretty good friends wit' Godiva, Whiskey. She was hangin' out wit' me an' da girls backstage after her concert at the Savannah Civic Center. She gets all o' her coke and weed from da Krew. She also mentioned how bad she wanna win dat competition, 'cause dat'll put her on da map. But she knows dat she'll need da votes o' da black community to help her out 'cause all o' da black folk is gonna place dey votes fa Gina Madison. In return, she say she gonna look out fa us country-ass ballers, ya feelin' me?"

"It's funny how white folks come callin' niggas when dey need favors, ain't it?" Whiskey answered Bubby through a cloud of exhaled marijuana smoke and noticed his smile cut upon hearing his answer. "Yeah, I know all 'bout Godiva. Matter o' fact, I remember when da bitch used to strip at da Strokers Club in Atlanta. I know all 'bout her big ambitions to be dat next Kelly Clarkson or Gwen Stefani. But tell me dis—Why should we help her? Why are you gonna go out on a limb to help dis white girl? How is it gonna benefit da niggas in da hood down here in da low bottom o' Souf Cack an' Georgia?"

"A'ight, bet. First off, I think I know Godiva just as well as you do, and guess what—I might even know a few things 'bout her dat you don't, such as her friendship wit' O'Malley's daughter Courtney. Those two are so close, if you didn't know any better, you'd swear that that they were dykes. But wit' da boys in da hood helpin' out Godiva in her music career, she has already promised to put a bug o' two in her girl's ear to back off da hustlas down here and back home in Peola. Ya man David probably forgot to tell you that da IRS tryin' ta get at 'im fa tax evasion an' some mo' legal shit. Snookey done told David dat he'd use his team o' lawyers to handle his case and pay off Uncle Sam for 'im, which should be finalized by da end of dis December. But after da IRS trial is over, Davey boy gonna have to start over from scratch, and in order him to get back up on his feet, he gonna need a whole lotta seed money, ya feel me? A whole lotta seed money and a hot artist to put Spanish Moss Records back on da map."

"Just like dat, huh? We help ol' girl win some dumb li'l televised contest, and dat karaoke will make everything all better, huh? Yeah, right."

"It don't matter none whether you believe me or not, 'cause da plan gonna go forward regardless. Yeah, you and me both couldn't give a flyin' fuck 'bout da goddam *Pop Star* competition, but plenty o' mufuckas do and a whole lot of 'em ain't nuttin' but a bunch o' kids. Kids wit' money all across dese United States who gonna buy up a shitload o' Godiva records once she wins dis contest over Gina Madison, which Snookey and dem already got locked down."

"I don't mean no harm or disrespect, but how da fuck you know Snookey gonna pay for all o' dis shit?"

"C'mon now, ain't you Snookey's son an' shit? You already know how Snookey do when it comes to bidness. Shit, half o' dem li'l rap niggas David got signed have relatives locked up down in Bloody Point Beach Penitentiary. Who you think put in da word to David to get dem li'l niggas inked to a contract?"

Whiskey steadily puffed on the blunt with a sense of nonchalance. "Dat's all good, Mr. Bubby, but how can you be so sho dat Godiva gon' live up to her part o' da bargain once she gets a record deal? After we big her up an' all, she sho as hell gon' blow up. Big time. Then where does dat leave us? Maybe back at da drawin' board, 'cause she ain't gonna need ya black asses no mo', ya feel me?"

"Dat ho know betta den dat. Shit, she ain't dat stupid." Latrice giggled.

"You know Godiva is Mayor Lattimore's niece an' Detective O'Malley's homegirl. Now Lattimore stays buyin' up coke from Peola's ballas from South Side, so he gonna get in da police chief's ear 'bout all o' dat hot police surveillance bullshit if Godiva say so. And she will, trust me. Godiva want this music career mo' den anything else. She already got CBS pullin' in a mufuckin' eighty-eight percent rating each an' every Friday dat da *Pop Star* show comes on. She knows she's on her way to much bigga an' betta things . . . if she gets da votes from all da black folks watchin' da show on Fridays. An' guess what, da niggas in dese country-ass ghettos gonna be her savior, 'cause wit'out dem makin' mufuckas call into the television studio, she might not beat Gina Madison, 'cause Gina's black, an' she knows dis. Godiva gonna win, and when she win da competition, we all know she gonna blow da fuck up. Bigger den Beyoncé, Britney Spears, Gwen Stefani, all o' dem otha bitches. She gonna do what the fuck da hood tell her to do, and dat's real talk."

"Shit, Godiva might look innocent to her fans an' dem celebrity judges, but dat li'l white bitch ain't nuttin' but a ho, for real. She done fucked most every rapper in Atlanta. Shit, she fuckin' ATL Slim right now, unbeknownst to David Ambrosia. Or maybe he know da shit but don't give a fuck." Mercedes snorted yet another long line of powder up her left nostril. "ATL Slim ain't the only one layin' pipe in her ass. I heard she give da goodies ta No Doubt's li'l young ass too. Guess she just can't get enough o' dat black dick."

Whiskey looked over toward Nicky, who was still visibly upset over Bubby's nonpayment. "Thanks for all o' da hospitality an' everything, but I gotta say one thing. I think dat it was fucked-up dat Nicky ain't got da money you owed him. He a betta man den me 'cause I'd o' done something 'bout it, not just sit here an' pout like a li'l bitch. Anyway, it's been a pleasure meetin' y'all." He got up from the couch amidst the hard stares of Bubby and his two mistresses.

"A'ight, Nick, I'm out. Catch you outside in the whip whenever you get done in here." Whiskey flipped Bubby his middle finger as he exited the fancy furnished trailer.

"Yeah, it's been real nice meetin' you too, smart ass."

When Nicky exited the mobile home and got into Whiskey's Jeep, he was immediately accosted by his homeboy, who was thoroughly disgusted by his embarrassing display in the presence of Bubby.

As they drove away from Bubby Smith's property, Whiskey began to formulate within his mind how he'd get Nicky's overdue money.

On September 17, 2005, the wind and rain was coming down in great blustery sheets, obviously the remnants of Hurricane Katrina. It was 12:48 AM on Hilton Head Island on a night not fit for man or beast. Whiskey sat in his Jeep Cherokee bobbing his head to an old mix tape of Snoop Dog and Master P while he applied a pair of black leather gloves to his thick hands and slid on a dark ski mask. The steady stream of rain pelted the Jeep like a million tiny drumbeats, causing snaking rivulets to cascade down the front and rear windshields. He removed a metallic blue SIG-Sauer P220 .38 caliber double-action semiautomatic from the drawer and admired the beauty of the powerful handgun as it glistened beneath the street lamps in his gloved palm. He then took the ten-round magazine filled with hollow-tip shells and slowly but firmly shoved it into place within the handle of the pistol.

Turning the key slowly, the engine of the Cherokee revved with the powerful peals of thunder that followed the bright flashes of lightning, its angry electrical fingers zigzagging hither and thither and illuminating the night sky.

Once along the road leading to Smith's cobblestone driveway, Whiskey saw, through the swift sweeping movement of the wiper blades against the blurry windshield, a single light glowing a yellowish white from the living room. It seemed to him that perhaps the trio were yet still up and at it. Grasping the weapon and tucking it down into his waistband, Whiskey exited the dry comfort of his Jeep's cabin and emerged out into the chilly, driving rain of the late-night thunderstorm.

With no guard dogs to worry about, the black-clad gunman sprinted across the cobblestone driveway and past the parked sports cars and artistically sculpted hedges with the ease of a shadow. Once on the porch, he took a moment to remove the rain-soaked ski mask from his head and shook his long braids free of excess moisture. Then he wrung the knit hat free from water and stuffed it into the back pocket of his loose-fitting jeans, figuring that he would have little use for it. He peered through the transparent flower-printed cloth of the lime-colored curtains and saw the naked bodies of the three lovers mingled together in a steamy embrace of lust-filled moans and rhythmic gyrations, seductive jazz melodies bumping in the background.

Steadying himself, Whiskey kicked in the door, which fell inward with a hollow metallic crash and sent the nude women screaming with terror behind the long, lean frame of their sugar daddy, who sat in wide-eyed shock as the gun-wielding home invader burst atop the fallen front door and into the living room. Without speaking, Whiskey squeezed the trigger and blasted away at the nude man sitting before him. Bright crimson splotches of gore splashed against the paisley-print wallpaper as several slugs tore through Bubby Smith's chest and abdomen, causing him to flop awkwardly face first on the plush carpet below.

While the dead hustler's blood seeped out into the khaki-colored fabric and spread beneath the corpse in a sickly purplish red circle, Whiskey continued on his murderous rampage by permanently silencing the two screaming women with multiple gunshots to their heads and upper body. The heavy peals of thunder and the downpour made the sound of gunshots inaudible, not to mention that no one in their right mind would dare venture out during a thunderstorm of such a fearsome magnitude as this one.

After he dispatched of the three, he took his time combing through the interior of the well-furnished home in search of drugs and money.

After a twenty-minute scavenger hunt through the various rooms, Whiskey returned to his vehicle soaked but with a plastic trash bag bearing several sandwich bags filled with marijuana, as well as four ki's of Colombian cocaine and over $224,000 in cash. He double-bagged the contents and couldn't help but smile broadly as he checked out the goods.

Bubby was, in his estimation, an egotistical blowhard who had really done little to further the cause of the

Fuskie Krew and seemed to care only about himself and his live-in tramps. No one would particularly miss his presence, and the police investigation that would begin within a day or so would end up going nowhere fast, due to the hood's unspoken code of silence when it came to cooperating with the boys in blue. Besides, he'd committed the murders during a driving rainstorm at the dead of night, and since he wasn't a citizen of the island, he would be miles away across state lines by the time the local cops launched their investigation. Nicky would be given the money owed him, and Whiskey would take the rest of the spoils with him back to Peola, where the real work would begin.

Three days later Whiskey treated himself and several of his friends to a party at the lavish upper-level VIP room of the 95 South nightclub. It was September 20, a night dubbed "Sexiest Stripper Showdown III," a much ballyhooed event that drew standing room-only crowds of booze-guzzling, cat-calling country boys intent on seeing an erotic parade of naked female flesh. While his homies from around the way enjoyed the risqué entertainment, Whiskey calmly sat at the bar and sipped on a glass of Grey Goose and cranberry juice, joking around with the bartender and laughing at the hilarious antics of the drunks in the audience acting a fool over the shapely dancers.

Unlike most others, Whiskey rarely, if ever, felt any connection with a murder he'd committed or any remorse for the victim or victims after it was over. He'd witnessed violent death since his early teens. He himself had once shot a Pakistani taxi driver in the face for calling his mother a whore and he was only thirteen. Scared straight programs, anger management counseling, church, and juvenile detention halls did little to sway the young thug from becoming South Peola's most lethal enforcer.

Whiskey swallowed down the remaining vodka and cranberry juice before sliding the empty glass to the side and picking up the newly prepared glass before him. He and the friendly old bespectacled bartender discussed the upcoming final competition of *Pop Star* pitting soulful diva Gina Madison against the surprising young songstress, Godiva. The men at the bar acknowledged that Madison's popularity within the black community throughout the country would continue to serve her well, as it had from day one, and that the sex appeal of the blonde bombshell could easily score a major upset at the end of the night.

Ironically, as nearly a dozen exotic dancers took center stage all at once, each girl stepping forward under the dazzling spotlights to display their unique individual moves to the raucous approval of the men, and a multitude of greenbacks tossed at their feet, Godiva's sultry rendition of Mtume's "Juicy Fruit" came blasting through the massive wall speakers.

Just then someone tapped Whiskey on the shoulder.

Whiskey turned to see the smooth, handsome face of Paul Ballard. "'S up, shawty?" He got up and embraced his childhood friend. "So you up in da club checkin' out da hoes, huh, pimp?"

"*Ssshhhheeetttt*, nigga, mufuck dese skank-ass bitches. I'm up in here ta holla at you, my dude."

"Is that right? A'ight, you got da flo'. Talk to a nigga, pimpin'."

Paul instructed the attentive bartender to serve him up

a stiff shot of straight Southern Comfort on the rocks and lit up a cigarette.

"You smokin' Salems again? Back in '02 you was on dem Marlboros hard. What happen? Dese joints better for you or somethin'?"

"Eat a fat dick, nigga." Paul handed the bartender a crisp twenty-dollar bill for a tall ice-filled glass of liquor. "Naw, when I was locked up in Akron, almost all o' da peeps in da pen smoked Marlboro, so I ain't had no otha choice. But once I got on da outside, I left dem joints alone."

"Why?"

" 'Cause dem mufuckas too damn harsh, dat's why."

Whiskey smiled and nodded in agreement. "I feel ya. If ya gon' kill ya lungs, shit, kill 'em softly. Ain't dat right?"

The young men shared a brief laugh then touched glasses in an impromptu toast to their long friendship.

"So you goin' to da telly wit' one o' dese tricks later on?"

Whiskey gulped his vodka and smiled slightly as he looked out over to the stage down below on the nude women writhing before the frenzied male mob. "Nope, I ain't pressed fa no ass, but I'm-a probably buy some pussy fa a coupla my li'l homies just ta show dem dudes some big homie love, ya heard me?"

Paul twirled his glass around gently as he gazed into it.

"C'mon, son, why you actin' all weird an' shit? You said you wanted to holla at me, right? A'ight den, speak on it, baby."

"True, true. You know dat big-money Bubby Smith got shot right?"

"Naw, son. You bullshittin', right?"

"Whiskey, c'mon now. I might joke around 'bout a lotta things, but when it comes down to talkin' 'bout da death of a boss playa like Bubby, I don't bullshit."

"A'ight, da nigga dead. An'? Dat's what happens in da game. People get kilt. Dat's life. I ain't really know 'im like dat no way."

Paul slowly slipped a swallow of his drink and turned around on his stool to watch the strippers.

"I only met dude like one time when I was down Hilton Head, but otha den dat, like I said, I ain't really know 'im too good."

Paul finished the Southern Comfort in one hard swallow then called out to the bartender for another glass.

Whiskey also asked the bartender for another round of booze, tipping the old man nicely in the process. "When did he die?"

"Three days ago, dey tell me. Dem boys down in da low bottom say somebody jacked his ass up in his crib, punished him and his two bitches, shot dem people multiple times an' ransacked da place lookin' fa shit. Dey musta found it too, 'cause all o' his money and dope was missin' when da po-po found 'em."

"Fa real? Damn, somebody musta really wanted him dead. Dat's why you gotta watch da kinda niggas you let up in da crib. You can't trust everybody, ya know."

"True dat, but you know as well as I do dat news travel fast on the streets. 'Specially down dey in low-bottom Souf Cack, niggas talk."

Whiskey calmly took his fresh glass of Goose, staring steely-eyed at Paul. "So what you sayin', Paul? Please tell me 'cause . . . sounds to me like you beatin' round da bush an' shit. Spit it out, nigga. Say what you came up in dis mufucka to say."

"You know dude was one o' dem Fuskie Krew niggas, right? You know he was one o' da most top-earnin' OGs down in the low bottom, right?"

"So what da fuck? He ain't nobody to me. Shit, I could give a fuck less if somebody kilt dat nigga's whole mufuckin' family, dawg! And why is you comin' at me wit' dis dumb shit? What you think, I had something to do wit' dat bitch-ass nigga? I know betta den dat, Paul. You got me fucked up, shawty. Whoever givin' you ya info, tell 'em ta come see me, a'ight. You tell 'em dat."

"C'mon, son, calm yo' ass down. I ain't sayin' shit 'cause, fa real, just like you, I don't give a fuck. How long we been knowin' each otha, Whiskey, huh? Since the third grade an' shit, right. C'mon, I always gotcha back— Don't you ever forget that shit either, ya heard me? But ya boy Nicky Stevens down dey spendin' up some shit like he just won da Beaufort County lotto or somethin', flossin' ice, pushin' a fresh new whip, an' some mo' shit. When asked 'bout his sudden long paper, he hollerin' 'bout how one o' his homies from Georgia peeled Bubby's cap back. So guess what, ya man mus' not be so used ta gettin' money like he just got, 'cause he sho nuff on some ol' hot shit, runnin' his mouf like an ol' bitch. Now feds an' everybody else payin' attention to his big-mouf ass. As you know, we here in South Peola been bootin' up wit' da Fuskie Krew for years now. Dem boys is our bidness partnas an' our peeps. Shit, Bubby might o' been a bitch, but he still a Fuskie OG, dawg. We can't let dat news get back to Joi 'bout who actually murked his homie, 'cause if it does, den you know dem Geechee boys gonna do all dey can to get back at da killas. Not only would he lose an important bidness partna, but you betta believe dere gon' be a interstate war in the street. Now I dunno 'bout you, but I ain't tryin' ta go back ta da days o' da ol' drug wars we used to have wit' da Jamaican posses when we ran wit' da Wreckin' Crew back in Souf Peola."

"Okay, you got me. I guess you just can't trust everybody, no matter how well you might *think* you know 'em—dumb-ass Geechee nigga."

"Yeah, you damn skippy. You of all people should know betta, Whiskey. Ya see, we been ballin' outta control since we been thirteen and fourteen, so we used ta havin' big dough. So we know how ta act when we get a big sco', but niggas who only used ta gettin' short money don't know how ta handle da big time, so dey make da block hot when dey do get dey hands on some real money."

"Yeah, you're right, Paul. I let my guard down, thinkin' dat I was helpin' a friend get what he rightfully deserved. It's all good, though. I'll slow his roll, all right."

After a few more stiff drinks, the well-buzzed pair returned to the lighter conversation of the *Pop Star* competition.

"Everybody know Godiva gonna win it all. She younger and prettier than Gina Madison. I mean, I like Gina's singin' style betta, but hey, I'd rather fuck Godiva though. I heard ATL Slim used ta hit dat all da time. Matter o' fact, he s'pose ta have an old underground mix tape wit' a single on it called 'White Girl,' where he talk 'bout how much he used ta fuck her. I betcha she got some good pussy. Whatcha think, Whiskey?"

"Oh fa sho. She built like a sista, so you know she got it goin' on in da fuck-a-nigga-real-good department."

While clearing the counter of empty glasses and coasters, the bartender chimed in, "Shit, I sho wish I could find out fa myself."

"Yeah, a whole lotta cats in da rap game either done hit dat or tryin' dey damnest to hit it befo' she gets married. Then again as a housewife, I s'pose." Paul smashed the smouldering butt of the cigarette into a glass ashtray.

"Godiva's fine an' all, but so is Alicia Keys and Beyoncé. Shit, you know you'd cross land an' mufuckin' sea to get either one o' dem dime pieces. Tell me you wouldn't."

"True dat, true dat, but I'm on some ol' jungle-fever-type shit in my life right about now, feel me?" Paul said.

"Hey, do you, my nigga. Sounds to me like you been listenin' to too much o' dat ATL Slim single. What's it called?—'White Girl,' or some shit?"

Paul nodded. "Yo' daddy Snookey claims Godiva's his nephew's baby mama an' dat her real name is Brandi Welsh, is dat right?"

"Yeah, she got a daughter by my cousin Rae-Kwan, an' yes, her name is Brandi Welsh. Most o' da old hands who ran wit' my pops an' dem back in da day remember Brandi. She just look a li'l different now 'cause she let her hair grow down to her ass. Dat's why she calls herself Godiva . . . 'cause o' her extra-long hair. I used ta go an' see her strip back when she danced at da Strokers Club in Atlanta," Whiskey said.

"Oh! So she was a stripper, eh? I thought so. 'Cause there's a hook in da song 'White Girl' dat start off like,

'a nigga stay flippin', trippin' and dippin',
makin' dudes sick from da fuckin' lyrics he spittin',
but check it, life got 'em vexed 'cause his bitch, she be
*   strippin'.' "*

"He musta seen her perform at da Strokers Club too. C'mon, it's one o' da most popular strip clubs in da South, if not da whole damn country, an' trust me, Godiva, or Lady Godiva as she was known on da stripper stage, was probably da only white broad strippin' at da Strokers Club. And she was, in my opinion, one of the most popular an' well-liked dancers in da whole joint, so it's easy for one of several dozen mufuckas to have laid eyes on her before." Whiskey handed the bartender forty dollars, buying a round of mixed drinks for them both.

"I fucks with ATL Slim though 'cause, not only can son flow, but he stays baggin' only da baddest bitches, dawg. Now dat's pimpology fah ya ass, ya heard?"

"Damn, nigga, hop off his dick fa once." Whiskey took a sip from his glass. "Of course, if you got a three-and-a-half-million-dollar record deal and puttin' out a new rap video every otha day, females gon' flock to you like moths to a flame. It's all a part o' da game."

"Yeah, but Godiva ain't just any ol' no-name groupie. She's a star in da makin'."

"Shawty, ya man ATL Slim a bitch, fa real. My pops used to be locked up wit' 'im befo' he got transferred outta Bloody Point Beach Penitentiary to anotha prison somewhere else.

"He hood an' everything, representin' Atlanta pretty good. He used to run wit' a gang called da Krazy Kountry Kripz, KKK, but when he called tryin' ta punk Snookey, he got dat ass whupped, damn near kilt, for real. So all o' dat shit he be spittin' on dem mix tapes, he ain't all thug, nor is da mufucka no playa like he say he is. So what, he got lucky an' fucked anotha celebrity. Dat ain't no real big feat or nothin'. Shit, I done had plenty o' famous chicks suck and fuck, an' I ain't no rappa or singa neither."

"Whiskey, man, you hatin' like shit, dawg. Give da nigga some props, man, c'mon."

"I just did. I said he was hood, but I ain't gonna suck his dick either. You talkin' 'bout dis dude like he God's gift to bitches or somethin'. Now dat right dere is some gay shit."

"Yeah, you hatin', bro. You sho nuff drinkin' dat *haterade*, ain't cha?" Paul slurred slightly from the deepening effect of the alcohol. Then he grinned. "Fuckin' a bitch like Godiva is a big plus fa a nigga's image. Ya see, it'll take you further along in da rap game. 'Specially fuckin' wit' a white bitch. Dat's just life. Why you think all da NFL and NBA stars got deyself a white woman on dey arm? 'Cause dey know she 'bout like a livin' Diners Club card or some shit. Hell, go back in ya history books an' check out Jack Johnson, America's first black boxin' champ. Shit, he was way ahead o' his time, 'cause he practically lived in white pussy. An' he ain't give a fuck 'bout what da white man thought 'bout it, 'cause couldn't no cracka whup his ass. And whenever he was in public or at home, he was strapped wit' da heat, ready fa any redneck feelin' lucky. Plus, he had money to burn, so mufuckas couldn't tell 'im shit. All dey could do was hate on 'im, and dat was 'round da early nineteen hunits. Now dat's what cha call *bossin' up*."

"Paul, you drunk, ain't cha?" Whiskey chuckled, then cleared his throat. "Godiva ain't trippin' off dat fake-ass wannabe trick daddy she engaged to. David Ambrosia a top-level record executive an' shit, so she might o' gave him a li'l bit o' ass back when she was strippin'. So what? And lemme tell ya somethin', Paul—At da end o' da day, a black woman gon' be da one ta have yo' back, nigga, don't you forget dat. Tonight dat liquor's talkin', but it's all right. I know you got mo' sense than dat."

Chapter 9

"We Own These Streets"

By October 1, Whiskey had a seventeen-year-old high-school dropout named Derek Myers pushing dope for him in both Hemlock Hills as well as the Badlands Manor projects. Paul Ballard had introduced Whiskey to a few crooked cops who would see to it that Whiskey's young drug courier would be able to sell his illegal wares without interference from other policemen or competing dealers along heavily trafficked strips of South Peola's drug-infested neighborhoods. They would also monitor his daily earnings, making sure that there'd be no underhand money or drug skimming, which often occurred whenever there was little or no supervision of the runners, particularly if they were of a tender age.

At 1:31 PM, Whiskey took the Peola commuter rail toward South Peola's Driftwood Station. By this time Derek Myers would be sittin' on the hood of his candy-apple red '65 Ford Mustang serving freshly cooked vials of beige-colored rocks to two, sometimes three, clients at a time as they stood in a winding line that stretched for nearly a block and a half, waiting to purchase their packages of fleeting baking soda-based nirvana.

Even though Whiskey frequented South Peola for business purposes, he had since lost the urge to mingle with the neighborhood thugs he'd grown up with. Most were a sorry bunch of losers who did little with their lives beside getting into trouble with the law and populating the surrounding projects with illegitimate children. A few others permanently crippled due to past involvement in gang warfare spent their days lounging around local pool halls, liquor stores, and barbershops, spinning colorful tales about gang banging experiences, all the while bumming loose change or cigarettes from anyone who'd give a listen.

Yet, the popular Hemlock Hills area barbershop, known to the folks in the hood as Eddie's, wasn't just a place to go to get a fresh shape-up or argue sports, but it served a slightly darker purpose as well. Edward Anderson, owner of the establishment, often used the shop as a front for a highly lucrative heroin and weapons ring that served all of South Peola and much of neighboring Savannah. Eddie also made a comfortable living as a loan shark, his ruthless techniques of punishing delinquent clients earning him the grim title, *Bonecrusher*.

Whiskey often ended up at Eddie's to have his beard trimmed neat and his silky hair taken out and freshly rebraided by Eddie's sister and co-owner, Ramona Anderson. Today was just that kind of a day for him to pay Eddie's a visit.

After he'd gotten his beard trimmed and hair braided, he met with Eddie downstairs in the shop's supply room to pay for a shipment of a dozen Israeli-made AK-47's and around $6,000 worth of heroin. He had just recently made a connection with a death metal guitarist from Savannah, by way of Orlando, who along with his band mates was big on smack. The AKs would be the weapon of choice in the Mickey O'Malley hit, which had yet to be organized properly.

The visit to his old South Peola stomping ground would end as it usually did—with him stopping past the 1300 block of Fenris and Pelco Streets to collect his weekly pay from Derek. The teenager as always had done exceptionally well that week, serving the blocks of Hemlock Hills and Badlands Manor a wide assortment of the best dope in town.

After presenting his personal courier as well as the kid's police overseers their portion of the drug money, Whiskey boarded the subway train with a plastic shopping bag filled with several stacks of rubber band-bound bills totaling $27,000, which he would take back home to place into a fire-resistant lockbox.

Around 6:30 PM he left his sister's home to meet up with a realtor to have dinner and a few drinks at Big Mama's Place as they went over paperwork and photos of several West Peola area homes he might be interested in purchasing.

Basically Whiskey had lived with his sister and nephews for the better part of two years, and though he and Tasha got along well, with the exception of her distaste for his choice of friends and baller lifestyle, he never wanted his involvement in the game to touch his family the way his father's drug dealing had claimed the life of his half-sister Dawn and his newborn nephew years ago. He knew that because he was so deep into the game that he'd have no choice but to distance himself in order to protect his sister and her kids.

Whiskey slowly flipped through the glossy printouts, intently staring at the lovely houses situated in several of West Peola's wealthiest communities.

As the middle-aged real estate broker rambled on and on in between bits of grilled swordfish steaks and sips of Parisian Chardonnay about the fine architecture and historical value of each house displayed on the photographs, along with the high-end amenities available in each, Whiskey feigned attentiveness to her, her words coming across as little more than vague babble. His heart was set on anything near the water, a lakeside rambler, a cozy beach house, or even a modest country cottage beside a woodland stream or lily-covered pond.

He quickly finished up his meal and assured his broker that he'd make his final decision by month's end as to which property he'd be buying and to begin the tedious process of signing the necessary legal paperwork.

From the time he'd arrived at the restaurant, and all through the meeting, his cell phone buzzed nonstop upon his waist. His two cop partners were attempting to speak with him about hooking up at Point Polite to talk business. (Point Polite was a popular park for nature enthusiasts, summertime picnics, and rich young lovers planning to make out in the backseat of the phantom.)

It was late, around midnight or so, when Whiskey pulled his Cherokee up beside the two police cruisers parked adjacent to the dark, silent picnic area and basketball court. He didn't trust cops and felt somewhat uneasy when he stepped out into the cool, breezy, autumn night to greet the boys in blue.

Hank Columbus was a wide, barrel-chested white boy with a square jaw, deep-set blue eyes, and a short-cropped military-style buzz cut. He spoke with a deep Southern drawl and couldn't have been much older than twenty-seven.

Maurice Tolliver was a six foot five former college basketball star who played shooting guard for the North Carolina Tar Heels. Born of Trinidadian parents, the deep-voiced, handsomely dark Tolliver had an eye for fashionable clothing and an obsession with grooming.

The two beat partners were like the odd couple, with Columbus enjoying all the niceties of redneck entertainment such as Monster Truck shows, NASCAR racing, and deer hunting, while the more refined Tolliver felt more at home flying out to New York to take in a Broadway show in Manhattan or playing a couple of holes of golf down on Hilton Head with members of his country club. There was one thing, however, that both men liked in common—illegal money, and lots of it.

"Well, well, look who's here finally. She musta been a pretty damn good fuck, 'cause we done called ya 'round 'bout a dozen times or so, I'd say. So did ya get your rocks off or what? You ol' horndawg, you," Columbus said in his heavy Southern drawl. "Then again don't answer that, bro, 'cause I haven't cheated on my old lady for a whole week and she's on the goddamn rag, for cryin' out loud. If I don't fuck something soon, I'm gonna have a bad case of blue balls. Say, ya think that hot sister of yours would be up for givin' a young studly white boy a shot o' ass?" he said, laughing out loud before spitting out a nasty, brown loogie as he chewed steadily on a plug of sun-cured tobacco.

Whiskey smiled broadly and flipped the cop the bird. "How 'bout you huggin' on dese nuts like ya mama done last night?"

The three men laughed at each other's expense for a few minutes longer. Then their conversation turned to business as they enjoyed a blunt that Maurice Tolliver had taken from the glove compartment of his police cruiser. Weed always seemed to be the perfect companion for any underworld business meeting, helping to sort of break the ice, particularly in uneasy contacts like this one.

"Ya boy Derek been ballin' outta control. I'll give 'im that much. He musta pulled in thirty-three gees just last month alone, but now that you've got the smack, I still think that you've got to have a tail on him, 'cause number one, this is too big of a deal to trust the boy, even Derek. Number two, he'll need protection just in case these cats wanna play hard ball an' the transactions goes south. So I'll make that ride down to Savannah to drop off the stuff to the metal heads, got it?" Maurice leaned up against his cruiser, his arms folded across his chest.

"He'll ride wit' Maurice in a unmarked car right after our duty shift is over 'round 'bout six in da evening. Think he'll be ready ta go by then?" Columbus took the blunt from his partner. " 'Cause that kid's slower than winter molasses sometimes, an' I don't know 'bout Maurice, but I ain't got no time for 'im ta be draggin' ass tomorrow."

"He'll be ready, trust me. He been pretty reliable fa me so far, an' dis'll be da first time he get ta go out from

Peola, since you been busy wit' Hemlock Hills and worryin' 'bout Chief O'Malley's actions on Fuskie."

Whiskey turned to meet Alonzo halfway along the
sidewalk. "Son, if you know so fuckin' much 'bout some
dude steppin' on my toes out Badlands Manor, why you
ain't do nothin' 'bout it?"

"I *am* doin' somethin' 'bout it. I'm tellin' you 'bout da
shit right now, ain't I? I got my own hustle I'm handlin',
but I got my ears to da streets all da time, so I hear things,
ya know? 'Specially things dat need ta be heard. So now
dat you know what need ta be done, you just need ta
make dese cats respect ya gangsta. It's just that simple."

Whiskey shook his head in frustration as he looked up
toward the fading warm golden light of the autumn
Georgia sky. "I'm gettin' real tired of all o' dis dumb shit,
dawg. It's just aggravation as a mufucka. Now I'm gon'
have ta go out an' murk another mufucka 'cause niggas
wanna violate an' shit. Damn!"

"Calm down, Whiskey. You fucks wit' Hank and dem,
right? Well, let da police handle ya dirty work fa ya. Ain't
dat what ya payin' fa?"

"You got a point there. Dat would be a good look,
though."

"You goddamned right, it'll be a good look. Why do
you put yaself in unnecessary situations when you don't
have to?"

"I'm gonna have ta get Hank's redneck ass ta do da job
'cause Maurice took Derek down to Savannah to drop off
some heroin to some new customers o' mine. I don't like
dat mufuckin' Hank too much, though. He too damn sar-
castic for me. Talk shit too much. Makes me wanna

punch him in the fuckin' face. But I guess he'll have to do for now," Whiskey said with disdain.

"Just think of it as bidness and bidness only, an' you'll be fine."

"Tell me some more 'bout dis Burt character, 'cause I ain't never heard 'bout him befo'."

"Like I said, all I know 'bout dude is dat he goes by da name Burt, or either Berk. I think it was Burt, though. He s'pose ta be up north, Newark, New Jersey, some say. He got a li'l crew pimpin' dat diesel an' shit out on da block from sunup to sundown, but it ain't nothin' da police can't handle."

"Ya know what? I'm gonna call Hank's hillbilly ass up in a minute so we can run up on this nigga tonight, catch his punk ass sleepin'."

"Tonight's as good a time as any to murk a mufucka. You can't miss 'im. My sources tell me he pushin' a hot pink Range Rover and he's always wearin' pink camoflauge hoodies and whatnot. So he can't be too hard to find out on da block. Plus, he be lettin' his li'l dope boys rock da pink too. I dunno, he's from Jersey, so he must think he's Cam'ron an' shit, huh?"

"Yeah, he probably do think he's Killa Cam. Too bad I'm gonna have ta wet his pink outfit all up." Whiskey checked the number of a call that had just come in on his Nextel. "I gotta go, dawg. Got some bidness to tend to, a'ight. I catch you a li'l later on."

"A'ight, bet, but a footnote 'bout my man Burt. Word on da street is, he's an informant fa Mickey O'Malley. Seems like ol' boy got a li'l bit suspicious 'bout da activities of several of his officers, 'specially da ones assigned to South Peola or, as Peola police department calls it, da

'Red Sector.' Some of O'Malley's top aides even know 'bout Burt's dope hustle, but they'd rather look da otha way when it comes to dirt on his own men, know what I mean?"

"Sonofabitch! So this nigga's eatin' from every angle, huh? Yeah, Alonzo, you right, somethin's gotta be done 'bout dis mufucka. An' quick!"

The brothers spoke for a brief time before driving away in different directions and with different objectives in mind.

By the time Whiskey arrived at Eddie's Barbershop in Hemlock Hills, it was around 9:45 p.m. Only Bone-crusher Eddie and Officer Hank Columbus were there, sitting back in separate barber chairs and laughing hysterically at the buffoonish antics of the skit characters on Comedy Central's *Chappelle's Show.*

Once he stepped foot into the dimly lit barbershop, it didn't take the two men long to show him why his presence was needed so quickly. The urgent phone call to him earlier had come from Bonecrusher Eddie.

Outside the shop, along the narrow trash-strewn alleyway, at the very end near the street corner, were the bloody, mutilated bodies of Burt "Jersey Boy" Johnston and three of his runners.

The two had pounced on the dope peddlers during the middle of the day, around noon or so, according to Officer Columbus, who puffed and passed a thick blunt among his partners. He and Bonecrusher Eddie related the details of the entire event, from the early-morning stakeout in an unmarked cruiser, leading up to the shakedown and arrests of the suspects, which ended with the subsequent murder of the four men and the gory dismemberment of their corpses.

Whiskey listened to the story as the cop and the loan shark accomplice worked in the old storage room, cleaning up the blood spatter, torn flesh, and bone shards that had been shattered wither and thither across the floor and walls by the bloodstained chainsaws that sat on top of a bloodied table that had clearly been used for the gruesome task.

The severed body parts were then meticulously placed into several large, heavy-duty garbage bags that were then tossed into the dumpster out back, from where it would be removed first thing the next morning and then driven some one hundred miles away to be taken by a tugboat-pulled barge, to finally end up far from civilization in a smelly seagull- and crow-infested landfill on Skidaway Island.

Chapter 10

"It Ain't Easy Being Gully"

"I-I don't know what to say. I'm like totally blown away right now. Thank you all so much for coming out and supporting me, especially all you guys at home who called in to vote for me. I love y'all. I thank God for giving me this gift. I want to thank the producers of *Pop Star*, the judges, and every single contestant who had the guts to come out and audition since January eighth up until now. You're all so very special to me. Wow! I want to thank and give congrats to Ms. Gina Madison for a wonderful final performance here tonight. Give it up for Gina, 'cause, girl, you ain't no runner-up. You're a bona fide star in the making, and with pipes like yours, you're well on your way to the very top.

"I'd also like to extend a very special thanks to my new producer and fiancé, David Ambrosia. I love you, sweetheart. And I want to say thank you for my lovely little girl watching at home. I know you couldn't be here tonight, baby, but I want you to know that Mommy loves you. And Mommy did it, baby, Mommy did it."

Seventy-five thousand strong roared their approval as a stunningly beautiful Godiva, adorned in a radiant form-fitting silver and sea-green satin gown shimmering with rhinestone embroidery, hoisted the star-shaped crystal and platinum trophy above her head after receiving well-wishing embraces from the show's host, judges, and dozens of defeated contestants surrounding her.

As was expected Godiva had surpassed Gina Madison by a walloping 180,000 phone-in and text-message votes to Gina's laughable 97,000 call-ins. But the masses that tuned into CBS's Friday night grand finale of *Pop Star* would never know the inner workings that launched the former exotic dancer into the stratosphere of superstardom.

About four months earlier on June 1, the IRS began to really step up its investigation of David Ambrosia's multi-platinum record label's books for tax evasion and fraud, among other financial discrepancies.

"Whiskey, I gotta let ya know, the feds are coming down on me real hard, brotha. So hard that I gotta either pay back all of the overdue money that I owe that IRS or go to jail. And you know that I ain't tryin' to do that. So, while I get up the cash to satisfy Uncle Sam, I'm gonna need somebody to run the business, ya know, handle the day-to-day activities of operating a record label. You can handle that, can't you?"

Whiskey was hesitant at first but quickly accepted his friend's offer, which was more of a cry for help than anything else. "You know I'm good for it, son. I got you," he said with reassurance.

Yet on this special night for America's newest singing sensation it wasn't her smiling, debonair multi-platinum producer fiancé who'd rendezvoused with her at her lavish suite on the sixty-sixth floor of Atlanta's towering Westin Hotel after leaving the festivities at the Georgia Dome. Instead his homeboy Whiskey agreed to see the lovely singer safely to her hotel room, since David Ambrosia had to meet with a group of important multimedia executives in Miami, Florida early the following morning in order to secure a summertime tour date for his suddenly famous lady friend for 2006.

It was a quarter past midnight when the tipsy twosome entered the fancy hotel room, which would serve as their love nest for a few hours until dawn.

Godiva threw open the large indigo-colored curtains to reveal a bird's-eye view of nighttime Atlanta, whose city lights twinkled brightly for untold miles below like a million fireflies. She then tossed her white ermine stole onto a nearby chair and plopped onto the king-sized bed, beckoning Whiskey with her finger, a naughty come-hither look in her gorgeous blue eyes. "I am sooo fuckin' wasted. How 'bout you? Are you nearly as trashed as I am?"

"Think I ain't? I musta kilt a whole fifth o' Crown Royal all by myself on top o' dat Rémy, so ya know I'm twisted like shit." Whiskey crawled onto the bed beside Godiva and took her into his arms affectionately.

"My ex-husband used to drink Scotch and water almost daily, but I couldn't stand the stuff. It tasted like paint thinner. It was fuckin' horrible. Maybe that's why we divorced."

"Naw, yo' ex-husband probably didn't know how ta tap dat ass right. Dat's why you had ta get rid o' his tired ass. Dat's what I think."

"Well, I will say one thing—Once you go black, you never go back. I'm one white girl that can attest to that one!"

Godiva's voice, though slightly slurred by a full night's worth of victory binge drinking, was still seductively sweet and breathy and had just enough of a Southern drawl to give a man an immediate hard-on. Whiskey always enjoyed Godiva's velvety singing voice even more than Beyoncé's or Alicia Keys, who were his favorite singers of all. The pop diva had surprisingly powerful range and depth for a voice as lifting and syrupy-sweet as hers. She had a unique almost uncanny way of taking someone's song, even from classy artists such as Bob Marley or Billie Holiday, and making it her own.

But now here in the privacy of a luxurious hotel room America's newly crowned sweetheart was taking turns sipping Cristal while cupping Whiskey's hairy testicles within her milky white fingers and slurping up and down upon Whiskey's shaft like it was an ebony sugar stick.

Whiskey palmed the top of Godiva's head as she slowly bobbed back and forth on his throbbing erection. He ran his strong, dark fingers through her silky golden blond mane as he threw his head back and groaned in ecstasy. He began thrusting himself forcefully into her pouting, red-painted lips. He felt his balls tighten with building semen and abruptly withdrew himself from his lover's mouth. He then moved around behind her, ripping off her white lace panties and aggressively shoving his meaty eight inches deep into her gaping pink slit.

"Ohh yeah! That's right, fuck me, baby. Fuck me hard with that big cock! I wanna feel you deep inside me. Yeah!! Oohh, yeahh, don't stop!!"

Whiskey had conflicting thoughts mingling inside his

head as he pounded the pop singer from behind. A small part of him actually hated himself for betraying his life-long friend. Had he been cheated on by any female he loved, she would have surely paid the ultimate price, along with her lover. There was little chance of him ever being a cuckold without seriously maiming or murder-ing the offending party. Yet, Godiva's ravishing beauty, delectable curves, and irresistible sex appeal had eclipsed any second thoughts he might have had of spurning her advances out of respect for his homie.

"Damn, you got some good-ass pussy, girl. Fuck! Keep it right dey. Ride dis big black dick. Dat's right, ride dis mufucka 'til I skeet off!"

The two intoxicated lovers moaned and groaned to-gether in a sweaty, orgasm-filled hour and a half of in-tense, animal-like passion before collapsing exhausted in each other's embrace upon wrinkled sheets.

After waking up from a brief catnap, a slightly hung-over Whiskey showered and left a soundly snoring Go-diva behind at the hotel. Not to be caught by snooping paparazzi, who would surely be waiting by the tens of dozens for Godiva to emerge from the Westin by the time the autumn sun peeked across the Atlanta skyline, he hopped into his whip at 4:57 AM and headed back to Peola.

It was almost ten when he pulled up into the driveway of his sister's North Peola townhouse. He entered the picket-fence home from the side and made his way down into the basement, which served as his personal space. His sister had long gone off to work, and his young nephews were by this time on a bus and on their way to school.

Before he could even get into the room and situate himself properly, his Nextel began buzzing loudly on his hip. It was the cops, Hank and Maurice, urging him to meet up with them at Big Mama's restaurant for a sit-down.

Whiskey showed up at the restaurant a little over an hour after the phone call feeling a bit grouchy from a night of boozing and marathon sex. The cops were seated at the far end of the crowded diner next to a large window, from where the Madison freeway with its bustling early-morning traffic could be seen and heard in the distance.

Whiskey took a seat at the table amongst the chuckling policemen, who carried on about the transvestite streetwalkers they'd busted the night before. With obvious disinterest in the ongoing dialogue, he ordered a cup of strong black coffee.

"Listen up, fellas, I know y'all ain't called me to talk 'bout a bunch o' fags y'all locked up. 'Cause, if so, I'm gon' drink my cup o' joe and I'm out da do'!"

"Calm down, calm down. We was just talkin' cop talk, that's all." Officer Columbus smiled brightly. "You look like hell, man. Musta been one heck of a party last night, huh?" Columbus nudged Tolliver, and winked at Whiskey in an effort to pry the details of his adventure from him.

"I didn't know I was being interrogated dis mornin'." Whiskey took the porcelain cup of steaming hot coffee from the waitress.

"Naw, just fuckin' with you, that's all. Seriously though, we got a bit of a problem down on Hilton Head. A problem that if not handled ASAP could ruin the whole Chief O'Malley hit thing we've all worked so hard to put together." Tolliver placed a collection of photos down on the table in front of Whiskey. "Seems like this cat in the da pictures done gone an' bumped his gums to way too many folks down in da low country," the redneck cop drawled lazily. "Nicholas Stevens, a.k.a. Nicky, has been down there spending money like water since mid-September, sayin' that you broke him off proper-like after you killed a certain Bubby Smith, who was obviously the head honcho down there or somethin', I s'pose. This kid's been tellin' people how you killed this douche bag an' then basically burglarized his house afterwards. Did you know 'bout that?"

Seeing the fury in the enforcer's tired bloodshot eyes, he shook his head and shrugged his broad shoulders.

"Hey, I feel ya pain, bro, but what can I say? Ya just can't trust everybody wit' a whole lotta cash, not even ya friends."

Whiskey slumped back into his chair and stared up at the slowly whirling ceiling fans above, exhaling a loud breath of disbelief and disappointment. Then he leaned forward, placing his beefy forearms upon the table, and stared at the police officers, who sat staring back silently from their respective seats.

"Y'all know what? I gave dat fool every bit o' da twelve hunit mufuckin' dollas he was cryin' 'bout. Chump change! Then, to make it worse, I murked dis nigga Bubby fa two reasons and two reasons only. One, 'cause Nicky's my homie, ya know, or so I thought, and two, 'cause dude was just a li'l too stuck on himself. And I can't stand dudes like dat. So, I goes over dis cat's house and he not only owed da boy money from a previous dope deal but he refused ta pay my man his bread. Plus, he disrespected 'im da whole fuckin' time in front o' me and his two hoes. So I took his ass out." Whiskey looked around the surrounding room to detect any eavesdropping on the part of the other patrons on the outside of their private booth.

Officer Columbus cleared his throat and smiled broadly. "Listen, Whiskey, I'm just as pissed-off about the situation as you are, but look, you got to keep ya voice down, okay. We in a restaurant, remember. But there's more. According to one of our contacts down in Hilton Head, he—Nicky I'm talking about now—was recently arrested outside of Bluffton, South Carolina for a simple DUI violation, but this idiot had a little over five thousand dollars worth of crack cocaine in the vehicle when they pulled him over.

"When they realized that ya so-called homie knew something about the September seventeenth triple homicide of Bubby Smith, Latrice Barton, and Mercedes Nolan, they took him in for questioning because, for the past few weeks since the murders, the Beaufort County sheriff's department been strugglin' to come up with clues to nail the dope man's killer. My sources tell us that he's being held in a Beaufort jail awaiting trial at the county courthouse on January fourteenth of next year. I don't need to tell you that he's already copped a plea deal to rat you and everybody else out 'cause those backwater cops down there don't really give a flyin' fuck about some drug dealer gettin' offed. They see it all the time, and frankly they feel like those Geechees are doin' everybody a huge favor, really. But now that Chief O'Malley has been hippin' the departments down there to the connections and delivery routes of the true movers and shakers of the dope game from Daufuskie Island all the way to Atlanta and Miami, having this guy take the witness stand in '08 would be disastrous, to say the least, for everyone concerned. And I do mean everyone. So regardless of how you may feel about this guy as a friend, he's got to be eliminated, period. I can't express to you the severity of this situation, feel me? I know that he's your friend from way back an' all, but hey, he's damn sure not thinking about you or your freedom at this point, right. Hell, if saving his own ass means bringing down his friends and business partners for a lighter sentence, a new identity, and a big pay-off, then so be it. I know it, and so do you. So with that said, I know that there's no other choice but to stop this kid from testifying against us in January. It's just that simple."

"Yeah, dude, we gotta get rid o' dis asshole, Whiskey. There's no other way," Maurice said.

Whiskey slowly but angrily flipped through the dozen or more photographs showing Nicholas Stevens in various stages of discussion with undercover officers in reference to the Bubby Smith murder, also known down in the low country as the Hurricane Katrina killings. Feeling the bitter sting of betrayal, a wave of revenge overtook him.

By the time the three men got up from the their booth, it was already decided that Nicholas "Nicky" Stevens would become yet another victim of the brutal backroads of the dirty, dirty South.

Chapter 11

"You Rat, You Die"

All too often criminals seem to forget the unspoken but ironclad rules of the game when reaping the benefits from the ill-famed trade. Unfortunately, such negligence of the laws of the mean streets brought to an end the career of many a hustler by way of a prison cell or a coffin.

At 11:16 AM on the morning of November 2, 2005, Nicholas Jared Stevens was found dead in his jail cell. The cause of death couldn't be immediately determined. Since he'd been housed in a private cell with the Beaufort County jailhouse, no other inmate could be blamed for his death, and with a twenty-four-hour police vigil, it was perplexing to the county sheriff's department how a perfectly healthy prisoner in his twenties could simply up and die on them out of the blue. A heart attack, maybe? Not likely. A stroke, perhaps?

Forty-eight hours later an autopsy on Nicky Stevens had confirmed that he'd been poisoned by an extremely lethal agent in either his food or drink the night before his untimely demise. This new revelation following the sudden passing of the county's most talked-about prisoner brought much unwanted press to the Beaufort County sheriff's department, which now had more than their share of questions to answer in the wake of this most embarrassing incident.

As the breaking news program interrupted a Thursday night college football battle between Palmetto State rivals, South Carolina and Clemson, Whiskey turned from tapping away at this computer to see his sister LaTasha descending the stairwell leading down to his basement apartment.

"What ya doin' down here, boy? Chattin' online wit' ya li'l cyber hoochies?"

"Naw, just checkin' out some o' dese houses my real estate agent e-mailed to me. I'm tryin' to decide which one I wanna get, 'cause dey all look nice, know what I mean?"

"Shit, if I were you, I'd take one o' dem beachfront homes, I guess, 'cause Mama used to take us to the beach every summer back in da day. Remember? We used to run up and down da boardwalk, bury each other in da sand."

"Yeah, an' get stung by dem fuckin' big-ass jellyfish."

"Whatever. You just couldn't sit ya li'l fast butt down and play in da sand. You had to wander off deep into da water. Shit, it's a wonder a shark didn't swim off wit' you." LaTasha leaned over her brother's shoulder to take in the photos on the computer screen. "You heard on da news 'bout Nicky Stevens gettin' poisoned, right?" She pulled up a swivel chair next to him.

"Hell, yeah. It's all over da news on every channel, even cable. Dat's real fucked-up, 'cause dat nigga was my son right dere. Know what I'm sayin'?"

"Yeah, I was pretty tight wit' 'im myself. I went to school with his sisters Tammy and Angela. I know one brother locked up for God knows how long, and now the other brother's dead. Dat's too much. Dat's why I keep tellin' you and dat hard-headed-ass Alonzo ta leave dem li'l hoodlum niggas alone.

"Just last week Friday I had ta get Peaches mind right, call herself goin' out da do' on a date wit' some li'l thug who pulled up in front o' da house beepin' his horn and whatnot. *Sheeeeit*, I waited good 'til she grabbed dem keys off da table, and I calmly walked myself right outside with her and introduced myself to mister man before I politely bid his fake Ja Rule-lookin' ass good night. See, maybe next time he'll have better manners for da next young lady he take out on a date. As for my daughter, he can chalk dat one up as a loss cause he ain't welcome here no mo'.

"See, most all of o' dem dudes y'all call friends an' whatnot ain't nothing but a bunch o' thugs and criminals. No way, you know da police don't respect 'em. Shit, dey probably da ones who killed Nicky, 'cause ain't no way in da world dem police gonna not know how dat boy ended gettin' poisoned. Dat's a bunch o' bullshit, an' dey know it.

"But, hey, dat's the price you pay fa fuckin' 'round out here on da streets sellin' dat dope and shootin' folks. Ain't no good gonna come from livin' dat gangsta life. I hope you an' Alonzo learn something from all o' dis. Ya do dirt, ya get dirt.

"Don't get me wrong, I'm real sorry 'bout what done happened to Nicky, an' I feel so bad fa his family, but Nicky was out dere hustlin' and wildin' out like da rest

o' dem, so I knew it wouldn't be but a matter o' time befo'
he got himself locked up or killed. It's a damn shame. He
was so young, had his whole life ahead o' him, and now
he'll be a meal for maggots. And for what? A li'l bit o'
money? Some jewelry? A fancy car or two? Y'all betta
wake the fuck up. Take heed and wake up."

Whiskey silently endured his big sister's scared-straight
speech, which usually followed the news of a friend's or rel-
ative's arrest, hospitalization, or murder from drug dealing.
He was tired of hearing the same I-told-you-so song and
dance over and over again and was ready to acquire his
very own digs pretty soon to avoid any further nagging.

The very next day he again met up with his police co-
horts who'd once more taken care of a potential threat to the
operation's smooth day-to-day affairs. The crooked cops related to Whiskey how they had gotten in contact with Beaufort Sheriff Oliver T. Drayton, a.k.a. "Doctor Buzzard," a
known cocaine and marijuana dealer among the area drug-
gies, as well as a renowned and feared practitioner of the
mystical hoodoo arts, the region's answer to voodoo.

It was rumored in and around Beaufort that the tall,
gangly country bumpkin was perhaps the only white
man to have been initiated into the magical brotherhood
of the Gullah people, and he utilized his dark arts to di-
rect malicious spells toward his enemies in the drug game
who had little, if any, protection against such super-
natural power.

Though the two Peola lawmen could've cared less
about the supposed paranormal prowess of their Carolina counterpart, they did respect and appreciate the
fact that Sheriff Drayton knew botany very well and

used a deadly combination of arsenic, belladonna and several other several of poisonous Sea Island plants to concoct a toxic brew called Graveyard Dust. This was then placed into a tall glass of sweet tea and served with a dish of smothered short ribs and mashed potatoes to Nicky Stevens, who dozed off about a half-hour later, never to awaken again.

Point Polite was rather quiet this particular afternoon, and the temperature outside was a mild seventy with a bright blue sky accented with thin white cloud wisps along the horizon, where a golden orange sun slowly hovered.

Officer Columbus sat behind the wheel of his squad car, lip-synching to a Lynyrd Skynyrd CD he was playing, while gorging on a box of KFC, while the always dapper Tolliver stood beside the squad car, sharing the details of the Stevens murder with Whiskey.

Whiskey eased a newly rolled blunt from the pocket of his hoodie and sparked it up. "So what y'all sayin' is dat ya man kilt Nicky wit' roots? C'mon, son, you soundin' like my gran'mama, wit' all dat hocus-pocus hoodoo shit. 'Specially comin' from a college-educated mufucka like you, Maurice."

"Look, I didn't say that I believed in any of the spells, hexes, or any of that hoodoo Geechee magic crap that Sheriff Drayton practices, but that stuff does involve a certain knowledge of botany as well as chemistry, to determine which plants are going to heal or kill someone. He's done it before, and as you can see in the case of Nicholas Stevens, he's obviously done it yet again."

Whiskey passed the smouldering blunt to the policemen beside him and shrugged his broad shoulders in disbelief. "I dunno, man. Dat's some weird-ass Stephen

King-type shit right dere. But how he gonna cover shit up, though? Everybody an' dey mama know my man done got poisoned. Now I heard da South Carolina District Attorney's office is gon' be lookin' into da case, so ya ol' hoodoo sheriff betta work some o' his strongest roots 'cause he sho nuff unda a microscope right about now. Him an' his whole fuckin' department. An' dat's not a whole helluva good look fa none o' us, ya feelin' me?"

Tolliver took in a final drag of the heavily packed blunt, smiling as he passed it over to his redneck partner, who snickered as if having knowledge of a joke that Whiskey was unaware of.

"Relax an' calm ya nerves, bro. We got it covered. Everythang's gon' be copasetic, okay. Now you just go on an' take it easy. We got dis." Columbus lowered the volume on his car stereo a bit. Then he tossed the empty box of greasy fried chicken bones over into a nearby metal garbage can. "We been dealin' wit Dr. Buzzard for well over, what, six years or so. An' he runs dat town wit' an iron fist, you hear me? An iron fuckin' fist. Everybody dat's anybody special in all o' Beaufort done bought pot or blow from 'im or else dey done went to him for some o' dem ol' hoodoo spells or whatnot, so you best believe ain't nobody down dere, white or black, rich or poor, young or old, is gonna rat out ol' Drayton. Everybody owe 'im somethin', for one thing, an' hell, most everybody else is too damn scared o' dat old bastard to dare run dere mouths to outsiders 'bout da sheriffs or his deputies. So you ain't got nothin' to worry 'bout, Whiskey, my man."

Whiskey took the blunt from Columbus's outstretched fingers and placed it to his lips. "Well, if y'all know dis so-called Doctor Buzzard like dat, den I guess everything's everything an' we can just keep movin' like always, huh?"

Columbus grinned. "Dawg, we're the police, remember? If there's anybody who can do the crime yet not the time, it's us, baby."

"Fa sho. Matter o' fact, I betcha if you was to, let's say, earn five bucks fa every dirty cop from, say, Key West, Florida all da way up north ta Boston, Massachusetts, *sheeet*, you'd be a fuckin' multi-millionaire," Maurice said.

Columbus pounded fists with his partner Tolliver.

"Shit, I'm damn near a millionaire now, white boy. Dunno what da fuck you talkin' 'bout." Whiskey chuckled.

"My bad, my bad, pimpin'. Please forgive me. Us li'l ol' po' white trash folk don't know too much 'bout ballin' and shot-callin'," Columbus answered.

Tolliver and Whiskey laughed heartily.

"Shut ya big redneck ass up an' pass dat blunt. How 'bout dat?" Whiskey playfully shoved Officer Columbus away as he attempted to embrace him. "An' fire up another one, 'cause you keep some good kush on you, Mr. Officer, sir."

On November 11, Whiskey stood in a long, black-clad file of tearful, sniffling men and hysterically wailing women, who slowly shuffled past the open casket displaying Nicky Stevens waxen corpse. As he drew closer to the shiny metallic gray he felt somewhat uneasy. After all, the dead man lying before him was indeed a friend for life, or so he'd thought.

Looking down upon his deceased friend's cold form, Whiskey thought he looked mannequin-like in his navy blue double-breasted suit and gray tie. He quickly moved on past the casket as several women bawled out mournfully behind him. Whiskey slowly walked over to the Stevens clan sitting along the front pew and weeping heavily. He offered a few words of encouragement to them then walked away down the church corridor, toward his vehicle parked outside.

The melancholy atmosphere coupled with the host of grief-stricken relatives and friends of the dead dope boy was enough to drive Whiskey away from the crowded Baptist Church. It was very uncharacteristic for him to feel guilt or a sense of remorse after a hit on an informant. But since he grew up knowing Nicky as well as he did, there was just no way to shake the sorrow and shame that now enveloped him in its dark embrace.

Driving across the scenic bridge that connected Hilton Head Island with the rest of mainland South Carolina, he could only think about the many times he'd spent nights over at Nicky's home enjoying the down-home Gullah cooking of Nicky's mother, Gertrude Ann Stevens, and the fun-filled sandlot football games played at Gator Field on Thanksgiving Day. The guy was like a brother to him, and he would still sorely miss him.

As he drove along the highway past rustic country homes and quaint old mobile homes, he listened to XM radio, silently recognizing that the deeper he got involved in the drug game, the more the bodies would pile up all over the low country regions of Georgia and South Carolina. And now with corrupt members of the Peola Police Department such as Office Tolliver and Columbus in cahoots with the area dope men, few ballers would be safe from the threat of death, not even himself.

Part II
Double Up

Chapter 12

"Blood Merger"

By December 14, David Ambrosia made another trip to Daufuskie's Bloody Point Beach prison to speak with the low country capo himself, Marion "Snookey" Lake. Although he had already secured a major record deal and a ten-city summertime tour for Godiva, he had taken a big-time hit from the IRS that left him nearly bankrupt, causing him to file Chapter 11 and to sell his record label to avoid prison. He had already asked Whiskey to run his business while he was going through his long, tiresome court proceedings of the past months, but had recently reneged on that idea when he found out about Whiskey's involvement with Tolliver and Columbus. He felt as though he could still manage the record label, now that his trials with the IRS had come to an end.

Now Ambrosia had arrived at the beachfront penitentiary to once more seek the aid of the drug lord. He sauntered down the hall, past armed guards, to the far end of the lobby to speak with Snookey.

Two corrections officers stood next to the seated Lake
Clan leader, cracking jokes and chuckling, while he
calmly sipped from a can of Mountain Dew at his favorite table in the corner.

Snookey patted an empty chair at the table, offering
his young visitor a seat. He already knew why Ambrosia
had come to see him. " 'S up, Dave? How kin I help you
today?"

Ambrosia pulled his chair closer to Snookey and cleared
his throat. "You probably know all about my trouble
with the IRS, right? Right, okay, check it out. After all the
money I had to pay out to the IRS an' my attorneys, I've
been pretty much wiped out financially. Now I'm not so
much worried about the money as I am about getting my
label back up and running. The feds are going to be in-
vestigating everything that I do from now on. I mean,
every fuckin' thing. So, with that said, I'm here to request
that you become a co-owner with me in the music business. I've got over twelve years in the industry, damn
near as much as I've put into the drug game itself. You already know yourself that I'm probably the fuckin'
hottest music producer in the States outside of Dr. Dre.
My beats are like mad sick, and my artists all make hit
records. All I need right now is a little seed money put
into my business account from a separate source. Because, if I even think about funneling interests into my
record label, Uncle Sam will ship my happy wigger ass
off to a federal penitentiary quicker than you can say
one, two, three."

"Partna-up wit' cha, huh? You know I'm good for it an'
all, but I can do but so much on lockdown here in da
sticks, baby. If I'm gonna be ya partna, I feel like I gotta

be a hands-on type o' nigga, ya know?" Snookey sipped on his drink.

David Ambrosia smiled weakly while shifting about in his seat. "Who says you gotta actually handle any of the technical legwork? All you have to do is put down the startup funds to get this party started again. Hell, you can use an alias. How about *Gullah Nation Records* or somethin'? Hell, I don't know."

Snookey snickered along with the C.O.'s at Ambrosia's title suggestions. Then he settled down and re-established eye contact with the music mogul. "Ya know, you just might be right, Davey boy, 'cause wit' dat dope money being laundered through yo' record company, it'll be da perfect smokescreen. 'Cause most o' da country know an' love you, 'specially back home in Peola. Spanish Moss Records? Are you shittin' me? Even wit' da tax evasion scandal, you still a music industry icon, an' a hometown hero nonetheless. So nobody will be the wiser 'bout what's goin' down behind da scenes, 'cept us cats in da game. You got me sold, white boy. Count me in."

"Now that's what I came down here to hear from you, Snookey. Because this is a win-win situation, dude. My fiancée Godiva's CD is due to drop on January twenty-second, and she begins touring with the rest of my artists during the summer. So you know that's sure money in the bank right there. Not to mention Godiva' friendship with new Peola Police Chief Courtney O'Malley. That can truly benefit every dealer, from Daufuskie to Miami. Because Godiva can pretty much get Courtney to do whatever she wants her to do, including have her old man Micky's sting operation halted down here in the low country."

The C.O.'s both smiled devilishly at each other before

staring down at Snookey, awaiting the drug lord's answer.

Snookey slowly curled a thick diamond ring on his index finger back and forth, beckoning the crooked guards over to his side, where he chatted in a low tone with his badge-wearing cronies, occasionally glancing over at Ambrosia.

After several minutes of intense discussion, the three men returned back to facing the calmly waiting Ambrosia.

Snookey said, "A'ight, you got yaself a deal. Da Lake Clan gon' put up da chedda fa ya and gon' pull da strings in da industry to put yo' girl on da map. Wit' da help o' da game, we gon' all ride da wave of her success straight to da top. Ain't dat right?"

"You know me. I'm going to make it do what it do, baby."

The men then raised up from their chairs and embraced each other warmly before Ambrosia disappeared down the long hallway and through the large doors beyond, the two prison guards trailing close behind.

Outside the iron wrought gates of Bloody Point Beach Penitentiary, the hip-hop mogul opened the door to his pearl-colored Hummer limo and slid into the plush backseat, where he popped open a cold bottle of champagne and poured himself a glass of the bubbly light gold beverage. He sank back into the soft moss-green leather, content with the knowledge that, once more, he would not only be back in the business of producing hit records, but he'd also be back on top of his game and better than ever. With the help of the game, of course.

* * *

It had been a month since twenty-seven-year-old Brandi Welch, a.k.a. Godiva, had won the much-ballyhooed *Pop Star* competition finale, walking away with the BMW 325Ci convertible, $500,000 and a major recording contract with Spanish Moss Records. Yet, the singing sensation's best friend, Courtney O'Malley, seemed to relish in carrying on her poppa's obsession with eradicating Peola's undesirables in his absence.

Daily police raids throughout South Peola's slums were the order of the day, many times harassing the innocent as well, simply for being relatives of targeted dealers. Aggressive racial profiling turned the projects into a veritable police state, bringing about the fear and loathing of Peola's finest to a new high amongst the ghetto's residents.

Whiskey and his numerous other area hot boys were furious at the cops with the latest rash of shakedowns, arrests, and even shooting deaths. It seemed as though Godiva had not spoken to her gal pal about the debt she owed to the streets, or either the policewoman simply didn't care.

Bright and early on November 28, seventeen Peola police squad cars roared up along Fenris Street in Hemlock Hills, sirens screaming and lights flashing. One by one, ghetto youth were shoved along the sidewalk and stuffed into the back of a black police Dodge Caravan while being read their Miranda rights.

"You little pricks are all gonna take a li'l ride downtown to my place. Got it? And once we're there, I'm gonna let a few of my guys, or should I say *homies*, kick it with you in our comfy little ol' interrogation room."

As the long row of frowning black teens shuffled past

her, fuming silently on their way into the back of the van, Courtney quipped, "Doesn't that sound like fun?"

One older teen said, "Why is you sweatin' us, shawty? We ain't even do nothin'. *Tsk, tsk,* man, dis is some bullshit!"

"First of all, you will address me as Chief O'Malley or Ms. O'Malley, not shawty. Do you understand me, *asshole*?" Courtney swiftly kicked the handcuffed youngster in the buttocks, sending him careening against a row of garbage cans sitting along the muddied patch of earth below. "Get his ass up on his feet and get him outta my fuckin' sight."

Two female officers went over to the prostrate youth, lifted him up from the muddied filth, and led him on up into the back of the van.

Shortly before the assembled cops drove away with their shackled quarry, the police chief turned toward the crowd of ghetto residents gathered along the curb and smiled as she surveyed the silent faces of hatred all about.

"Let it be known that this is a new day in Peola, Georgia, people. No longer will thugs, hoodlums, and dopers overrun this fine town with their poison and crude manners. Nor will I or my department stand for any noncooperation on the part of you citizens in regards to our follow-up investigations. Got it? And so help me God I'll do everything in my fucking power to bring every single criminal scumbag to justice by any means necessary, just as my dad instructed me to do. I'll be back here tomorrow, and the day after that, and the day after that, and as long as it takes, until you folks down here in South Peola finally realize that it is us, the Peola Police Department, not you, who truly rule this city."

With those parting words, Courtney O'Malley and her accompanying officers drove away from the crowded streets with their dozen or so arrests.

Whiskey questioned Ambrosia as they sat in the front office of Spanish Moss Records. "Man, what da fuck is goin' on wit' cha girl Courtney?"

The hip-hop mogul shrugged his shoulders while sighing deeply. "Man, I dunno what to tell you, Whiskey," he said after handing over a stack of papers to the attractive Asian secretary, who stood waiting patiently before exiting the spacious office through the heavy glass double doors.

"I know for a fact that Godiva and I both met with Courtney for well over two hours at her place out in Canterbury Arms. The three of us discussed over dinner what was expected of the department in regards to having a blind eye and a deaf ear as far as any drug trafficking conducted by our individual organizations, namely Peola's Bad Boyz II Syndicate, which is our homies right here in town, as well as your dad's Lake Clan, and also Joi Steven's Fuskie Krew, which is a part of the larger Geechee Gullah Nation that comprises of several other cliques down in South Carolina's low country.

"So, as far as I'm concerned, everyone that I just named is pretty much immune to any and all police harassment here in Peola, as well as down in South Cack. So relax, okay? I know how much of an asshole Courtney's old man was and is, but hey, she's her own person. She's already given us her word that she would take care of us.

"Now Godiva and Courtney go way back. They were friends since junior high, so Godiva knows her better than anyone of us. And she has promised me that Courtney O'Malley is a woman of her word who'd do anything she asks because they're more like sisters than mere friends. And my fiancée doesn't lie. She knows how the guys on the grind went to bat for her to gather up votes throughout minority communities across the country for her to win *Pop Star*. She hasn't forgotten, because she speaks about it every single day. She is grateful, and I myself will make sure that she does everything in her power to bless the streets back every chance she gets. So do me a favor, Whiskey. Work with me and give Captain Courtney O'Malley a chance, will ya?"

Though he nodded in agreement with his homie's assurance of the new police chief's compliance, Whiskey still had his doubts about the Irishman's daughter.

Just before midnight on November 29, Whiskey was slowly cruising East Peola's King Boulevard, in the direction of Burginstown Mall, to catch a movie and have dinner with a young lady he'd been wooing for the past week. The familiar sight and sound of a police Crown Victoria showed up in his rearview mirror, causing him to cuss out loud in anger and frustration as he pulled over to the shoulder of the busy street.

With words of assurance spoken softly to his suddenly nervous date, Whiskey turned to meet the bright glow of a flashlight pouring in the open driver's side window.

"Is dere a problem, officer?" He squinted as the bright light drew closer, illuminating the entire whip.

"License and registration please, sir," the cop demanded.

Whiskey's girlfriend asked with a sharp tone of irritation, "Is there a reason why you pullin' us over?"

"Ma'am, I suggest that you simply sit still and shut your mouth before you happen to piss me off more than I am already. Okay?"

The girl unlocked her seatbelt and leaned across her host, yelling out the window into the flashlight's cold white beam, "Well, that's sounds like a personal problem to me, officer, because I know my rights. And you just can't go around stopping people without them knowing why they're being stopped."

The rude cop then demanded that both parties exit the vehicle. After a profanity-laced request for an explanation, the couple were promptly frisked and, following a routine search of Whiskey's vehicle, immediately arrested.

Two twenty-dollar bags of weed were recovered, along with a semi-automatic handgun with a full clip in the paper-cluttered glove compartment. The two were cuffed, read their Miranda rights, and transported back downtown to the Peola Police precinct for booking and interrogation.

During the uncomfortable and humbling ride downtown to the police station, Whiskey sat silently fuming, while his lady friend loudly ranted and raved about the treatment from the arresting officer, who egged the enraged girl on.

Whiskey and his now exasperated date were released from the city jail at 9:48 the following morning, after his brother Alonzo paid $1,000 bail, which Whiskey didn't have on his person at the time, carrying only several major credit cards in his billfold.

For over three hours, Whiskey had been grilled non-stop by a trio of straight-laced, no-nonsense detectives, who came down on him like a ton of bricks. Knowing the ways of the dope game like he did, the street-savvy baller remained mostly calm through the bulk of the questioning.

In the end he refused to answer any further questions until he spoke with his lawyer. That, however, turned out to be unnecessary, because no formal charges were ever filed, which meant that there would be no future court date concerning the late-night arrest.

As November gave way to December, Whiskey had had enough of Chief Courtney O'Malley's traitorous behavior and had devised a method to slow her roll. He met with Columbus and Tolliver. As Bonecrusher Anderson looked on from the high perch of one of his barber chairs that swiveled around slowly, the three men debated back and forth about blackmail and bribery.

"Looka here, y'all," Whiskey said, "I dunno what da fuck's wrong wit' y'all's boss lady Courtney, but she's trippin'. An' I'm talkin' 'bout some hardcore trippin', son. Now David my dawg an' all, but his fiancée seem to be mo' concerned wit' her music career right now dan tellin' her li'l Irish girlfriend to chill out with all o' dat Robocop type shit. So I'm gon' have ta go raw gutta my damn self, ya feel me? Since nobody seems to wanna stop dis bitch, I ain't got no choice.

"I got a couple o' pictures o' Godiva butt-naked on da stripper stage back when she used ta dance at da Strokers Club in Atlanta. I know good and damn well dat she gonna want da American public to know nothin' 'bout dat. Know what I'm talkin' 'bout? Not to mention, some more shit I got on her. So y'all two betta get dat li'l bit o' info out to ya boss if she so much of a friend to miss bigshot Godiva, 'cause, don't forget, if it wasn't fa my pops an' dem, dat bitch wouldn't be a star right now, ya feel me? So she need to get her shit together befo' da *National Enquirer* get a hold o' some nude pics, a'ight."

"Look, man, I know Chief O'Malley is just as hardcore as her father when it comes to nailing drug dealers, particularly those identified with your dad Snookey. Those two plain just hate each other, so you gotta believe that his little girl's not going to have much love in her heart for Lake Clan types either," Officer Tolliver responded dryly. "You know we got ya back in whatever you want done, don't we, Hank?"

"Oh, no doubt, Bub, no doubt. Hell, I don't like Courtney O'Malley either. I'd fuck her, but I don't like her." Columbus chuckled from having one can of Coors too many.

Whiskey lit the end of an apple-flavored Black & Mild cigar as he sat amongst his crooked pals. "Anyway, I spoke to my pops yesterday and he really want us to turn up da heat on dat Fuskie Island bidness, ya know? David done told me dat he don't want Godiva to get involved in none o' dis thug shit we got goin' on 'cause it'll fuck her career up at this early point. Shit, I ain't mad at 'im. Godiva is his meal ticket to get back on da map, know what I'm sayin'?" Cigar smoke rose lazily above Whiskey's corn-rowed head.

"That may be true," Tolliver said, "but what I don't like is that Courtney, er, Chief O'Malley, I mean, calls herself handling the bulk of Godiva's scheduling and day-to-day appointments, so she basically manages the girl.

David seems to be fine with it also. And she has been in constant contact with her father down in the Big Easy about her dealings with local drug dealers here in Peola as well as continuing his operation down on Daufuskie Island."

"Yeah, she straight trippin', bro, but she don't know shit 'bout da hit dat's gonna go down on her dear ol' dad," Columbus chimed in with his distinctive Southern drawl.

Whiskey steadily puffed on the smoldering stogie as the other men chattered about the murder plot of Micky O'Malley when he arrived again on Daufuskie from his sojourn in storm-torn New Orleans.

"Don't Snookey got a bunch o' dem Geechee boys to peel ol' Mickey's wig piece back?" asked an intoxicated, red-eyed Bonecrusher Anderson, who was lying back in a barber swivel chair and clutching a forty-ounce of Colt 45 malt liquor in his thick hand.

"Fa sho, pimpin'. You know how Snookey roll. He got a couple o' like hardheads posted up ta put in work, know what I'm sayin'. But befo' we kin get shit on an' poppin', we gon' need ta pick da most gulliest, grimiest thugs from da island ta punish dis cracka, feel me?—No offense, Hank."

The brawny copy snickered. "No offense taken, bro. Hell, I ain't nothin' but a red-necked, beer-guzzlin' wigger, so trust me, Whiskey, I ain't hardly mad at cha."

"A'ight, bet. Anyway, Snookey wanted me ta come down to Fuskie ta get dese Geechee niggas' minds right, so dey kin do dis job da right way, feel me? My nigga, Doctor Buzzard, done wired me thirty grand ta take some time-off down on Fuskie, ya know?"

The hoodoo-practicing sheriff had built up quite a

profitable narcotic ring over the past decade himself and could ill afford to allow the Irishman to destroy that, so he was more than happy to bless Whiskey with the "vacation money" he needed to take care of this pressing matter. I'm-a need some time to whip dem dudes inta shape, 'cause dey real raw an' shit, an' dey ain't never had ta do nuttin' like dis befo'. So, yeah, I'm-a go down dere an' make it happen, cap'n."

Tolliver smiled broadly as he poured himself a clear glass of Jack Daniel's and Coke, swirling the potent, brown nectar around with the ice-filled glass before downing it in one grimacing gulp. "I really want this caper to go as smooth as possible. I still think that Godiva is more concerned with her upcoming concerts than with offing the sire of her best friend. So I've contacted some friends of ours who serve on the Beaufort County sheriff's department. You see, Whiskey, I too have spoken with the good Doctor Buzzard. He's already got two rogue cops working for us down on Daufuskie who will get as much info on O'Malley's fat ass as possible so that we can organize this hit properly. Get it?"

Everyone nodded in agreement to the crooked cop's words.

Tolliver continued as his interested friends looked on, "By early January, Mickey O'Malley will be back in South Carolina from New Orleans, so we've got to act fast because it's nearly December right now. There's this cat name Lonnie Newhart, a.k.a. Moose. He's a local high-school football legend down there in the sticks, but now he's much better known for flipping bricks than for touchdowns. It's this guy who'll be helping us in our efforts to eliminate Mickey O'Malley.

"Before O'Malley arrived down on Daufuskie, Moose was earning anywhere from fifty-five to sixty grand per week selling coke from Hilton Head all the way up to Richmond, Virginia, and down past the Florida Keys. It's rumored that he also ruled the low country with an iron fist, murdering over fifty-eight rival drug dealers in the fall of two thousand.

"My good friend, Lieutenant Gordon Nasser of the Savannah City police department, met Moose back in ninety-eight and has done brisk business with the guy ever since. I personally did my homework on the guy, and I found that he had connections with the Medellín and Cali Cartels in Colombia, not to mention various drug cartels out in Mexico, and even heroin smugglers from as far away as Afghanistan. The boy's a true baller, and trust me, he doesn't take kindly to some lard-ass mick cop ruining his coke business. Besides, he's also an ally of your dad. You did know that, didn't you, Whiskey?" Tolliver eyed Whiskey, who sat in a barber chair directly across from him.

"Who don't work for Snookey? Everybody dat's anybody out here on da grind done worked wit' my pops at one time or another. I don't put niggas on a pedestal just 'cause dey done made a li'l bit o' cheese from slangin' birds an' shit, 'cause if you 'bout yo' work out here on dese streets an' you ain't bullshittin', you gon' eat. All I'm tryin' ta do is get at dis bitch-ass O'Malley, so everybody kin breathe easier, sleep betta at night, and continue to serve dese fiends and make dis money like we always been doin', ya heard me?"

Tolliver glanced over at Columbus, who shrugged his shoulders nonchalantly as he channel-surfed the shop's overhead television with a small silver remote.